Joyce Grenfell

George, Don't Do That . . .

&

Stately as a Galleon

Illustrations by John Ward

HODDER &
STOUGHTON

George, Don't Do That . . . text copyright © 1977 by Joyce Grenfell
Illustrations copyright © 1977 by John Ward
Stately as a Galleon text copyright © 1978 by Joyce Grenfell
Illustrations copyright © 1978 by John Ward

George, Don't Do That . . . first published in Great Britain in 1977
by Macmillan London Ltd
Stately as a Galleon first published in Great Britain in 1978
by Macmillan London Ltd
This omnibus edition first published in Great Britain in 2005
by Hodder & Stoughton Ltd
This paperback omnibus edition published in Great Britain in 2006
by Hodder & Stoughton Ltd
A division of Hodder Headline

The right of Joyce Grenfell to be identified as the Author of the Work and the
right of John Ward to be identified as the Illustrator of the Work has been
asserted by them in accordance with the Copyright, Designs and Patents Act 1988.

7

A CIP catalogue record for this title is available from the British Library

ISBN 978-0-340-89637-2

Typeset in Sabon MT by Palimpsest Book Production Limited,
Polmont, Stirlingshire

Printed and bound by Clays Ltd, St Ives plc

Hodder Headline's policy is to use papers that are natural, renewable
and recyclable products and made from wood grown in sustainable forests.
The logging and manufacturing processes are expected to conform to
the environmental regulations of the country of origin.

Hodder and Stoughton Ltd
A division of Hodder Headline
338 Euston Road
London NW1 3BH

Contents

George, Don't Do That . . .

Stately as a Galleon

George – Don't Do That...

Six Nursery School Sketches

and

'Writer of Children's Books'

Foreword

The original idea for the Nursery School sketches began in a radio series, the 'How' programmes: a collaboration between Stephen Potter and myself. In 1944 we produced 'How to talk to children', and in it was the first brief draft of what later turned into a full-length sketch called 'Flowers'.

I had never been in a Nursery School, but I was always aware that most of us change our manner and our tone of voice when we speak to infants. Try saying to a very small child: 'Who's got beautiful new blue shoes on!' and I think you will find that you have put on a special voice that you would not use to talk to people of your own size.

My father was the only person I ever knew who addressed babies in prams as if they were his contemporaries. He spoke as he would to a bank

He spoke as he would to a bank manager.

manager or a bishop; friendly but respectful. I never saw a baby turn away or wince. Sometimes a tiny eyebrow may have been raised, but a look of interest took over and the pleasing pink blob of a small face registered relief and rapport.

Even as a child I noticed the way those in authority spoke to the rest of us, and I could reproduce it to amuse my fellows. I marked the sarcastic note that one teacher relied on. She was surface-jolly, had favourites and her sarcasm had bite. I observed this with some disdain. You

Mrs Bowthorne and Miss Chugwell.

couldn't trust Mrs Bowthorne to be fair. Miss Chugwell, more secure in her relationships, drew from her class of eight-year-olds a readier, more generous response. She didn't need weapons to buoy up her ego. She spoke low, without pleading.

Children's toys, games and clothes, hairstyles and language change; so do their names – Wendys, Pixys, Nevilles and Normans have currently given way to Shirleens, Sandras, Rocks and Waynes, but their unpredictable observations, discoveries and individualities, continue, thank heaven, to surprise, confound and delight.

Talking to three-to-five-year-olds presents different problems, but as far as I can see authority's voice is still what it always was: bright, bluffingly calm, cheerful, encouraging and occasionally desperate. It

3

is that bright teacher-tone of voice that needs to be added to the printed word of this collection of scripts.

For the script of 'A Writer of Children's Books' please hear a tone less desperate and wholly confident – her sales are astronomical. She is unaware that what she writes is not Eng. Lit.

John Ward's drawings are not portraits of Sidney, George, Hazel, Susan and the rest. None of them is identified, but their kind is.

Joyce Grenfell
1977

To all who cope in nursery schools

NATIVITY
🌿 Play 🌿

Hello, Mrs Binton. I'm so glad you could get along to see a rehearsal of our Nativity Play! Can you squeeze in there? I'm afraid our chairs are a wee bitty wee, as they say north of the border!

Now then, children. We are going to start our rehearsal. Where are my Mary and Joseph?

That's right, Shirleen, take Denis by the hand

Mary and Joseph were friends.

and come sit nice and quietly on this bench in the middle.

Oh, you're a cattle, are you?

Don't drag him. He'll come if you leave him alone!

Don't hit each other, Mary and Joseph were *friends*.

Now, who are my Wise Men?

You're a Wise Man, aren't you, Geoffrey?

Oh, aren't you? What are you then?

Oh, you're a cattle, are you? And you are going to low. Splendid! Go over to Miss Boulting, will you, please?

Miss Boulting ... You are organising the animals and the angels? He is one of yours.

Now, my Wise Men here, please!

Billy, Peter and George.

And George, Wise Men never do that . . .

Now my Kings, please.

Of course, Mrs Binton, we know that by tradition the Wise Men and the Kings are one and the same, but we did want everyone in our Nursery School Nativity Play to have a chance, so we have taken a few liberties, and I don't think any one will mind.

Now Kings: Sidney, Neville, Cliff and Nikolas Anoniodes.

Four Kings, I'm afraid. We happen to have four lovely crowns, so it seemed a pity not to use them. Sidney, put your crown on straight please, not over one eye. What have you got under your jersey?

What have you got under your jersey?

That's not the place for a hamster, is it. Put him straight back in his little pen, please.

Sidney, which one have you got, Paddington or Harold Wilson?

Well, who's got Paddington?

Neville, put him back at once.

Poor Paddington and Harold Wilson, it isn't very Christmassy for them under your jersey.

Sidney, I think it serves you right if Harold Wilson bit you, and don't bite him back.

Because he's smaller than you are. Are you bleeding?

Then don't make such a fuss.

Cliff, put your crown on, please.

It's too big? Let's see. Ah, yes it is . . .

Where are you! Oh, there you are! Nice to see you again! Change with Nikolas.

Nikolas, you can manage a big crown, can't you? You've got just the ears for it.

I think if you pull your ears down a bit that will hold it up. And lean back a bit. That's it.

Stay like that, dear. Don't move.

Wise Men and Kings, don't muddle yourselves with each other.

Now then, Shepherds.

Jimmy, you are my First Shepherd and not a racing car.

Yes, Caroline, you're a shepherd.

No, dear you can't wear your Little Bo-Peep costume: because there aren't any little girl shepherdesses in our play. They're all boy shepherds, and you are a girl being a boy shepherd.

Little Bo-Peep.

Yes, it is rotten. But we just have to settle for it. I think if you are very good perhaps you can wear a lovely grey beard; wouldn't that be fun?

George, what do Wise Men never do?

Yes . . .

Jimmy, do you remember what you see up in the sky? Something lovely, isn't it?

Do you remember what you see up in the sky?

No, not a baby. Try again.

It's a lovely silver star, and you are going to put your hand up and point to it. And what are you going to say when you do that?

No, Sidney, he isn't going to say, 'Please may I go to the bathroom?'

I think perhaps next year we might make do with a Christmas carol.

Children, that isn't funny; it's a perfectly natural function, and we might as well get used to it.

Come on, Jimmy. You are going to say, 'Behold!' aren't you?

Yes, you are, dear. You said it yesterday.

You'd rather say it tomorrow?

Perhaps you are right.

We have broken the back of the play, so you may as well get ready to go home. Hand in your crowns gently, please. No, Sidney, you can't wear your crown home on the bus.

I think – I HOPE it will be all right on the night.

But you know, Mrs Binton, I think perhaps next year we might make do with a Christmas carol.

Flowers

Children – we're going to do our nice 'Moving to Music' this morning, so let's make a lovely fairy ring, shall we? And then we'll all be flowers growing in the grass.

Let's make a big circle – spread out – wider – wider – just finger-tips touching – that's it.

Sue, let go of Neville –

Because flowers don't hold hands, they just touch finger-tips.

SUE. Let go of Neville.

And Sue, we don't want GRUMBLERS in our fairy ring, do we? We only want *smilers*.

Yes David, you're a smiler – so is Lavinia – and Peggy and Geoffrey. Yes, you're *all* smilers.

Yes, you're all smilers.

QUIET, PLEASE.

Don't get so excited.

And Sue is going to be a smiler too, aren't you Sue? That's better.

George – don't do that . . .

Now then, let's all put on our Thinking Caps, shall we, and think what flowers we are going to choose to be.

Lavinia? – What flower are you?

A bluebell. Good.

Peggy?

A red rose. That's nice.

Neville?

A bluebell. Good.

A *wild* rose. Well done, Neville!

Sidney? – Sidney, pay attention, dear, and don't pummel Rosemary – what flower are you going to choose to be?

A *horse* isn't a flower, Sidney.

No children, it isn't funny, it's very silly. If Sidney can't think of a better flower than that we'll have to go on to someone else until he can.

Now then Sue, what are you?

Sidney, pay attention, dear.

Another rose! Oh I *have* got a lovely bunch of roses, haven't I? Peggy is a *red* one and Neville is a *wild* one, so I expect you are a beautiful *white* one, aren't you?

Oh, you're another red one! I see . . .

Now then Sidney?

A carrot *isn't a flower*, Sidney. *Think* dear, and don't blow like that. How about a tulip?

A holly-leaf isn't a flower, Sidney. All right, you'd better be a holly-leaf.

Now, children, listen very carefully.

Elvis, stop bouncing, please.

No, bouncing isn't dancing, Elvis. Don't argue, dear – just stop bouncing. You watch the others – you'll see.

When Miss Boulting plays her music I want you all to get up on to your tipmost toes, light as feathers and dance away all over the room wherever the music takes you. And remember: you are all lovely flowers in the grass.

Everybody ready?

Just a minute, Miss Boulting.

Sidney – come here, please.

What have you got in your mouth?

What have you got in your mouth?

I can't hear a word you're saying, Sidney, so go out of the room and spit it out, whatever it is, and then come back and tell me what it was. And Sidney. Both feet. Don't hop.

Now then, children, we're not going to wait for a boy who puts things in his mouth like a baby – we're going to be lovely flowers growing in the grass, and the sun is shining down on us to make us grow tall and beautiful and – Geoffrey, stand up – flowers don't look backwards through their legs, do they?

Flowers don't look backwards through their legs.

What flower are you?

A fat daisy! Good.

Hazel, what do we do with our heads?

We hold them up.

I should think so.

Come in, Sidney!

COME IN. There's no need to knock the door down, is there?

Now what did you have in your mouth?

It can't have been nothing, Sidney, because I distinctly saw something.

Yes, I know it's nothing *now* but what was it *then*?

A big button! Well, I'm very glad you spat it out, aren't you?

You didn't? Do you feel all right, Sidney? Sure? Well, get back into your place, then.

Incidentally, where did you get the button?

Off Rosemary's pink frock. I'm ashamed of you, Sidney, a big boy of four to go around eating buttons off little girls' frocks. What flower are you going to be? I've forgotten. You'd better be a hollyhock.

No, you can't be a *super-jet*, and if you are going to be a crosspatch you'd better go and sit down over there till you are a nice boy again. You can be thinking what flower you are going to be. Go along . . .

George – what did I say before? Well, don't . . .

No, you can't be a super-jet.

23

Come along, children. Listen carefully to the music and then dance like a flower to it.

We're ready at last, Miss Boulting. I'm so sorry.

One – two – Off we go.

Dance, Neville, don't just stand there. Dance.

Head up, Hazel, and use your arms.

Peggy, dear – don't forget to breathe.

Rhythm, George. And cheer up – you're a *happy* flower, George.

Yes, you are.

Because I say so.

Oh good, Sidney, I knew you'd think of something.

All right, you shall be a cauliflower – only be it *gently*.

We're ready at last, Miss Boulting.

Free Activity Period

Oh, hello, Mrs Hingle. I'm so glad you could come along. As you see, we're just having a Free Activity Period, and in our Free Activity Period each little individual chooses his or her own occupation. Some are painting, some are using plasticine, and some work at a sand-table. We feel that each little one must get to the bottom of his or her self and find out what he really wants of life.

Who is making that buzzing noise?

Well, stop it please, Neville.

Hazel, dear, come away from the door and get on with your plasticine.

I love to see them so happily occupied, each one expressing his little personality . . .

George – don't do that . . .

Now, children, I want you all to say 'Good morning' to Mrs Hingle. Good morning, Mrs Hingle.

No, Sidney, not good-bye. Mrs Hingle has only just come. You don't want her to go away yet?

No, she hasn't got a funny hat on, that's her hair.

So sorry, Mrs Hingle. Sometimes we ARE just a trifle outspoken. We try to encourage honesty, only sometimes it doesn't always . . .

And this is my friend Caroline, and Caroline is painting such a lovely red picture, aren't you, Caroline? I wonder what it is? Perhaps it's a lovely red sunset, is it? Or a big red orange?

It's a picture of Mummy! For a moment I thought it was a big red orange, but now you tell me, I can see it is a picture of Mummy.

Aren't you going to give her any nose?

No nose.

It's so interesting the way they see things.

Sidney, don't blow at Edgar, please.

I know I said you could choose what you are going to do, but you cannot choose to blow at Edgar.

28

Say 'Good morning' to Mrs Hingle.

Because it isn't a good idea.

Yes, I know it makes his hair go up and down, but I don't want you to do it. Now get back to the sand table, there's a good boy.

Yes, there is room, Sue; there's heaps of room. Just move up a bit.

Susan! We *never* bite our friends.

Say you are sorry to Sidney. You needn't kiss him.

No, you needn't hug him. Susan, PUT HIM
DOWN.

No fisticuffs, please.

She hasn't made any teeth marks, has she,
Sidney?

Well then . . . don't fuss.

Free activity.

*Sometimes our little egos are on the big side, I'm
afraid . . .*

Hazel, dear, I don't want to have to say it again:
please come away from the door.

Why can't you?

Well, you shouldn't have put your finger in the keyhole, and then it wouldn't have got stuck.

Children, there is no need for everyone to come and have a look just because poor Hazel has caught her finger in the keyhole. Back to your work, please.

No, Sidney, I don't think it is stuck in there for ever and ever.

I don't for one minute think we will have to get the Fire Brigade to come and take the door down to set her free. You do exaggerate, Sidney.

Well, if we haven't got her finger out by dinner-time she'll have to have it here.

And her tea.

And her supper and stay the night.

But we are going to get it out, aren't we, Hazel?

David. Turn round, please, David. Right round.

Use your hanky, please, David.

And again.

And again.

And now wipe.

Thank you, David.

Hazel, why did you put your finger in the keyhole?

To see if it would go in!

Well, now let's see if we can get it out!

Who is making that buzzing noise?

Neville.

And now wipe.

I know you are a busy bee, but boy busy-bees don't buzz. Only bee busy-bees buzz.

I can still hear you, Neville.

Neville!

I should think so.

He's such a musical child, and one doesn't want to discourage him.

Sidney, take that paint-brush out of your ear and give it back to Lavinia.

Yes, you do want it back, Lavinia. You like painting.

Yes, you do.

We're hoping she is going to take to it soon.

Now then, Hazel, have you tried wiggling it?

You know, Mrs Hingle, this child's finger really

This child's finger really is caught in the keyhole.

is caught in the keyhole . . . I think the Fire Brigade are the best in an emergency. Yes, there is a telephone – at the end of the passage. Would you? Oh, that is good of you. I'll stay here and hold the fort and prepare the children. Thank you so much.

Children, I don't want anyone to get excited, but kind Mrs Hingle has gone to see if we can get one of those clever men from the Fire Brigade to come and help us get Hazel's finger out . . .

Oh, you've got it out, Hazel. Well done. That's lovely.

IT'S ALL RIGHT, MRS HINGLE – SHE'S GOT IT OUT.

Sidney. You are not to go near that keyhole. SIDNEY.

Can you get it out?

I SPOKE TOO SOON, MRS HINGLE . . .

Oh, Sidney . . .

Story Time

Children . . . pay attention, please. Free time is over, so put away your things and we are going to tell our nice story, so come over here and make a circle on the floor all around me, and we'll tell the story together. We've got a visitor today, so we can tell our story to her.

Will you be all right there, Mrs Binton? I think you'll get a good view of the proceedings.

Hurry up everybody. Don't push – there's lots of room for us all.

This group story-telling is quite a feature of our work here in the Nursery School, Mrs Binton. We like to feel that each little individual has a contribution to make to the world of make-believe, and of course many valuable lessons can be learned from team work. We're a happy band of brothers here!

Edgar, let go of Timmy's ear and settle down.

Come along, everybody.

Sidney, come out from under the table and join in the fun.

No, you're not in a space rocket.

You can't wait for the count-down, you come out now.

Don't you want to help us tell our nice story, Sidney?

Then say, 'No, thank you.' And stop machine-gunning everybody, please.

And Neville, stop being a train and sit down.

All right then, get into the station and then sit down.

George . . .

No . . .

Let's have some nice straight backs, shall we? What shall we tell our story about today?

Rachel, take your shoe off your head and put it on your foot.

Shall we tell it about a little mouse?

Or a big red bus?

And stop machine-gunning everybody, please.

About a dear little bunny rabbit! All right, Peggy, we'll tell it about a dear little bunny rabbit.

No, Sidney, he wasn't a cowboy bunny rabbit, and he didn't have a gun.

Why don't you come out from under the table and help us tell our nice story?

All right, stay where you are, but you must stop machine-gunning everybody. I don't want to have to tell you again.

One of our individualists! He does have little personality problems, of aggression, but we feel that when his energies are canalised in the right direction he is going to be a quite worthwhile person. That's what we hope . . .

Where did our bunny rabbit live?

No, he didn't live in a TV set.

No, not in a tree.

No, not in a flat.

Think please.

He lived in a HOLE.

Yes, Hazel, of course he did.

Only some of us call it a burrow, don't we?

He lived in a burrow with – who? His mummy bunny rabbit . . . and his? . . . Daddy bunny rabbit . . . and all his? . . . dear little sister and brother bunny rabbits. Wasn't that nice.

Yes, it was, Sidney.

No, Sidney, he wasn't a burglar bunny rabbit. Nor was his daddy. He was just an ordinary businessman bunny rabbit.

David, don't wander away like that.

Yes, I know the window is over there, but you don't want to look out of it now. Our story is getting much too exciting. Come and sit down by Neville.

Neville, don't pull your jersey down over your knees like that; you'll get it all out of shape.

Geoffrey, Lavinia, don't copy him. I don't want everybody pulling their sweaters down over their knees.

I don't want everybody pulling their sweaters down over their knees.

Now then, Peggy, you tell us, what was our bunny rabbit's name?

Yes, I know his name was bunny rabbit, but what did his mummy call him, I wonder?

Well, Piggy bunny isn't a very good name for a bunny rabbit. You see a piggy is a piggy and a bunny is a bunny, so we can't have a piggy bunny, can we?

Nor a pussy bunny.

Nor a doggie bunny.

Nor an elephant bunny.

Let's be sensible, please.

No, Sidney, Silly Old Fat Man isn't a good name for a bunny rabbit.

41

Nor is Wizzle Wuzzle.

No, it's not as funny as all that. There's no need to roll about on the floor.

Timmy, what have you got in your hand?

But we haven't had toast and marmalade for two days. Where did you find it?

In your pocket. No you can't eat it – it's all fuzzy. Now don't touch anything. Go and put it in the waste-paper basket and then wash your hands.

Peggy open the door for him. *Don't touch anything* and hurry back, please; we need you.

Timmy, what have you got in your hand?

Now then, Hazel, what would you like our bunny rabbit to be called?

Yes, I think Princess Anne is a very pretty name, but I don't think it's a very good name for a boy bunny rabbit. We'll call him Billy Bunny Rabbit . . .

Because that's his name . . .

Well, because I happen to know. We're not going to discuss it any more.

Sue don't kiss Neville like that.

Because he doesn't like it.

Yes, I know you like it, but he doesn't.

I don't know why he doesn't like it, but he doesn't.

No, and you can't go under the table and kiss Sidney, because he doesn't like it either.

Well, you didn't like it yesterday, Sidney. You must learn to make up your mind, mustn't you?

George . . .

Lavinia, you tell us what our bunny rabbit was doing all day.

He was riding a horse, was he? That is unusual for a rabbit, isn't it? I expect he went gallopy-gallopy, don't you.

Oh good, Sidney, you are coming out to help us tell . . . no, Sidney, you cannot go gallopy-gallopy . . .

Neville, Susan, Peggy . . . everybody . . . come back here at once. You cannot go gallopy . . .

Sidney, come back here.

You know, sometimes I don't think love is enough with children.

You cannot go gallopy-gallopy.

Sing-Song Time

Children, we've had our run around the classroom, and now it's time to start our day's work. We're going to have a sing-song together, and Miss Boulting is going to play for us, so come and settle down over here, please.

Kenny, why haven't you taken your coat off?

No, it isn't time to go home yet, Kenny! You've only just come.

You'd rather go home? Bad luck.

No, you can't go, not quite yet.

Kenny, you've only been here about ten minutes. Come and sit on the floor next to Susan. You like Susan.

No, Susan, I don't think he wants to sit on your lap.

No, Susan, I don't think he wants to sit on your lap.

No, I thought he didn't.

Kenny! We don't want to see your tongue, thank you.

No, not even a little bit of it. Put it back, please.

All of it.

And give your jacket to Caroline, I'm sure she'll hang it up for you.

Thank you, Caroline.

Who is that whistling?

Sidney, you know we never whistle indoors. You can whistle in the garden, but we never whistle indoors.

Yes, I know you have just whistled indoors, but don't do it any more.

And don't punch Jacqueline.

I'm sure she didn't say she liked you punching her, did you Jacqueline?

Well, I don't think it's a good idea, so we won't have any more punching.

He is rather a disruptive element in our midst, Miss Boulting, but he does try to belong more than he used to, so we are encouraged, bless his heart.

Let's be *kind* to each other today, shall we? We are going to learn some more of the Drum Marching Song we began yesterday.

Who remembers how it starts?

No, David, it doesn't begin 'Twinkle, Twinkle Little Star'. That's another song.

Yes, I know you know it, but we aren't going to sing it now.

No. Not today.

And not tomorrow.

Drum Marching Song.

I don't know when.

We are going to sing our Drum Marching Song now.

Edgar and Neville, why are you standing on those chairs?

You can see into the fish-tank perfectly well from the floor. Get down, please.

No, Neville, you can't hold a fish in your hand.

Because fishes don't like being held in people's hands. They don't like coming out of the water, you see. Their home is in the water.

Well, they do have to come out of the water when we eat them, but these aren't *eating*

Fishes don't like being held in people's hands.

fishes. These are *friend* fishes. It's Phyllis and Fred. We wouldn't want to eat Phyllis and Fred.

No, Sidney, you wouldn't.

I don't think they'd be better than sausages.

Come back, please. You don't have to go and see Phyllis and Fred. You know them perfectly well.

I don't know what they are doing behind the

weeds, Sidney. Just having a nice friendly game, I expect.

Neville, you tell us how the Drum Marching Song begins.

Yes! That's right.

'Rum tum tum, says the big bass drum'. Well remembered, Neville.

When we know the song well we're going to march to the Drum Song. But today we'll just stand and sing it; so, everybody *ready*?

'Rum tum tum, says the big bass drum.'

Just a minute, Miss Boulting.

Where is your drum, Kenny? No, not on your head. It's in front, isn't it, on a make-believe string round your neck.

Sidney, I heard what you said. You know it isn't 'Rum tum tummy'.

It may be funnier, but it isn't right.

Yes, it is a funny joke. Let's get the laughter over, please.

Finished?

Now then. Ready?

Thank you, Miss Boulting.

'Rum tum tummy . . .'

Yes, I made a mistake. It was silly, of me, wasn't it? Yes, very silly.

Sh – sh –. It wasn't as silly as all that.

I think we'll go on to the next bit perhaps . . .

Miss Boulting . . .

'Rooti-toot-toot, says the . . .'

Who says 'Rooti-toot-toot', David?

No, David, not 'Twinkle Twinkle'.

Yes, Lavinia, the '*Cheerful* Flute'.

And what is a flute?

No, Dicky, it isn't an orange.

It isn't a banana.

It isn't an apple.

It isn't FRUIT, it's FLUTE.

FLUTE.

And what is a flute?

Yes, Lavinia, it's in a band. It's a musical instrument in a band. And how do we play it?

No, we don't kick it and bash it about, Sidney.

Now think.

We *blow* it.

Yes, Edgar, we *blow* it, and the music comes out of it. It's a musical instrument, and we *blow* down it.

Rachel, don't blow at Timmy.

And Timmy, don't blow back.

I'm sorry she blew you a very wet one. But don't blow a wet one back.

Now use your hankies, and wipe each other down, both of you. I'm sure you're both sorry.

No, Kenny, it isn't time to go home yet.

Shirleen, why are you taking your skirt off?

Timmy, don't blow back.

I'm sure Mummy wants you to keep it nice and clean, but you won't get it dirty from singing, you know.

Yes, it is very pretty.

Yes, and it's got little doggies all over it. Little blue and little pink doggies. Put it on again, please. Yes, your panties are pretty; *and* your vest.

But pull down your skirt now.

George. Remember what I asked you not to do? Well, then . . .

'Rooti-toot-toot, says the cheerful flute.'
Rest.

Sidney, you're whistling again. And if you are

going to whistle you must learn to do it properly. You don't just draw in your breath like that, you have to blow in and out.

It's no good saying you bet I can't whistle, because I can. I've been able to whistle for a very long time, but I'm not going to do it now. But I can.

I don't know why I compete with him, Miss Boulting. I really shouldn't.

Let's start our Drum Marching Song from the very beginning, shall we?

One, two . . .

What did you say, Miss Boulting?

Already! So it is. Oh, good. And here is Mrs Western with our milk and biscuits.

Get into a nice straight line by the trolley, please.

No, Kenny, it isn't time to go home yet. There is still an hour and a half to go . . .

Here is Mrs Western with our milk and biscuits.

.... that chairs don't pin him against the wall with it.

We're hoping she'll get at our good neighbour policy here, Mrs Binton, but it doesn't always ....

Neville, please don't dismantle ...... the ....., there.

Going Home Time

(It is winter)

Children — it's time to go home, so finish tidying up and put on your hats and coats. Some of our mummies are here for us, so hurry up.

Billy won't be long, Mrs Binton. He's on hamster duty.

Now let's see if we can't all help each other.

Janey — I said help each other. Help Bobbie

carry that chair, don't pin him against the wall
with it.

*We're having a go at our good neighbour policy
here, Mrs Binton, but it doesn't always . . .*

Neville, off the floor, please. Don't lie there.

Don't pin him against the wall with it.

And Sidney, stop painting, please.

Because it's time to go home.

Well, you shouldn't have started another picture, should you. What is it this time?

Another blue man! Oh, I see, so it is.

All right, you can make it just a little bit bluer, but only one more brushful, please, Sidney.

We don't think he's very talented, but we feel it's important to encourage their self-expression. You never know where it might lead . . .

Rachel. Gently – help Teddy *gently* into his coat.

It's a lovely coat, Teddy, what's wrong with it?

Oh. It looks like a boy's coat when you wear it. And lots of boys wear pink.

Poor wee mite, he has three older sisters!

Neville, I said get up off the floor.

Who shot you dead?

David did? Well, I don't suppose he meant to. He may have meant to then, but he doesn't mean it now, and anyhow I say you can get up.

No, don't go and shoot David dead, because it's time to go home.

George. What did I tell you not to do? Well, don't do it.

And Sidney, don't wave that paint-brush about like that, you'll splash somebody. LOOK OUT, DOLORES!

Sidney! . . . It's all right, Dolores, you aren't hurt, you're just surprised. It was only a nice soft brush.

It's all right, Dolores, you aren't hurt, you're just surprised.

But you'd better go and wash your face before you go home.

Because it's all blue.

Sidney, I saw you deliberately put that paintbrush up Dolores's little nostril.

No, it wasn't a jolly good shot. It was . . . I don't want to discuss it, Sidney.

Now go and tell Dolores you're sorry.

Yes, now.

Thank you, Hazel, for putting the chairs straight for me.

You are a great helper.

Thank you.

And thank you, Dicky, for closing the cupboard door for me.

Dicky, is there somebody *in* the cupboard? Well, let her out at once.

What did you go into the cupboard for?

Are you all right, Peggy? What did you go into the cupboard for?

But we don't have mices – I mean mouses – in our toy cupboard. Mouses only go where there is food, and we don't have any food in our toy cupboard.

When did you hide a bicky in there?

Every day!

Well, perhaps we have got mices in our toy cupboard. I'll have to look.

No, you go and get your coat on.

Dicky – We never shut people in cupboards.

Because they don't like it.

What do you mean, she's puggy? Peggy's puggy?

Oh, she's got puggy hands. But you don't have to hold her hand . . .

Well, you must ask her nicely to let go.

Well, if she won't let go . . .

You'll have to work it out for yourself, Dicky.

Edgar and Timmy – your knitted caps are not for playing tug-of-war with. Look, now the pom-pom's come off.

Whose is it?

Well, give it back to Sidney.

Where are your caps?

Well, go and ask Sidney to give them back to you.

Turn round, Geoffrey. You've got your wellingtons on the wrong feet.

Yes, you have. You'll have to take them off and start again.

Why can't you reach?

You've got your wellingtons on the wrong feet.

Well, undo your coat and then you can bend.
Take off your woolly gloves.

And your scarf.

You can keep your balaclava on. How many
jerseys are you wearing?

Heavens. No wonder you can't bend.

Caroline, come and help Geoffrey.

Don't kick her, Geoffrey. She's come to help.

Sidney, I told you to put that paint-brush down
. . . LOOK OUT, DOLORES!

Well, *that* wasn't a very good shot, was it? You
didn't mean to put it in her ear, did you?

Well, you shouldn't have.

You're all right, Dolores. It was just a bit of a
surprise, but you'll have to go and wash again.

Because you've got a blue ear.

Sidney, I'm ashamed of you, a big boy of four, and she's only just three.

And Sidney, what have you done with Timmy and Edgar's caps?

No, I'm not going to guess.

And I don't want to know they are hidden in a special secret place, I want to know exactly where they are.

No, I'm not going to try and find them. You're going to tell me where they are.

Well, go and get them out of the waste-paper basket at once. Waste-paper baskets aren't for putting caps in.

Now go and say you are sorry to Dolores.

Yes, again.

We think his aggression is diminishing, but we do have setbacks.

Lavinia, is that your coat you've got on? It looks so enormous.

Oh, you're going to grow into it. I see.

Hazel, thank you for helping Betty into her jacket.

Just zip her up once. Not up and down.

No, Neville, you can't have a turn.

No, children, you can't all zip Betty.

Jenny, come here.

Jenny, when we have paid a visit to the littlest room, what do we do?

*Jenny, when we have paid a visit to the littlest room,
what do we do?*

We pull our knickers up again.

Good-bye, Hazel, Good-bye, Bobbie. Good-bye,
everybody.

Good-bye, Mrs Binton.

Hurry up, Sidney, because you'll keep your
Mummy waiting.

Well, your Granny then.

Somebody is coming to take you away, aren't
they, Sidney?

Good.

No, you won't see me tomorrow, Sidney.

Tomorrow is Saturday, thank heaven.

Writer of Children's Books

Writer of Children's Books

(*The scene takes place in the book department of a large store, where an author has been autographing copies; and now she is going to talk to her young readers.*)

Hullo, boys and girls.

I was so pleased when you asked me to come along and tell you how I write my books for children.

Well, of course, the answer is – I don't. No, my books write themselves for me.

I think we are all Little Ones at heart, aren't we, grown-ups?

Yes, even the Growly Bear Daddys at the back!

And I don't believe I have ever grown up, and I think perhaps that's my secret. That, and the fact that kiddies come first with me.

Well, as you know, children, I write lots and lots of books for you, and this is how I set about it.

First of all I go upstairs to my Hidey-Hole – well, this is really just a great big upstairs work-room but I like to call it my Hidey-Hole.

I pin a notice on the door and it says, 'Gone to Make-Believe Land'. This is just my way of saying, 'Please don't come and bother me, because a book is writing itself for me, and we mustn't disturb it, must we?'

Then I put a clean white sheet of paper in my typewriter, and I sit down in front of it, and I close my eyes.

And what do I see?

I see a rambling old house in Cornwall.

And I hear seagulls – and I see children – one – two – *three* children – scrambling up the cliffs, because they are very nearly late for tea.

And their names are Jennifer-Ann, and Robin-John, and the little one is called Midge – because he is the littlest one.

Oh yes, he has a proper name. It's Anthony Timothy Jeremy Michael, and he doesn't like porridge – but we won't tell anyone, will we?

And I sit there, and I type and I type, and as I do so I learn all about Jennifer-Ann's unruly mop of red curls, and her way with hedgehogs.

And about Robin-John, who is more of a fish than a boy – you should see him dive from the top diving-board.

And all about their father – kindly, overworked, sunburned, twinkling Dr Merryweather.

Then all of a sudden it's dinner-time, and I rub my eyes and I find myself back in my Hidey-Hole – and look! – a great pile of typed pages on the table beside me.

They must have written themselves while the story told itself to me.

And so I go on till a book is made.

And then I start another one.

This time it's a rambling old house in Yorkshire, and I hear sheep-bells, and I see children – three children – and their names are Sara-Mary,

75

Jonathan-Christopher, and the little one is called Tiddler – because he is the littlest one.

It's always the same with me.

No, I never rewrite, and I never read what I have written.

But you children do, millions and millions of you children do, and that is my great joy.

And it is my husband's great joy, too.

He has given up his work to encourage me in mine.

We have made Hidey-Holes for each of our five children so that they, too, may learn to let books write themselves for them.

And my husband has his own Hidey-Hole – where he adds up.

Well, I think it is time I got back to my Hidey-Hole, don't you?

'Stately as a Galleon'

and other songs and sketches

For Laurier Lister

Foreword

I was brought up on story-telling. My mother was a gifted mimic and an imaginative inventor of stories, and my brother and I sat entranced while she made up adventures and acted them out for us. (I wrote about this in my first book of memoirs, *Joyce Grenfell Requests the Pleasure*.) Ruth Draper, a close family friend, performed her monologues for us in our nursery from the time when Tommy was four and I was rising eight. (I've written about this, too, in the same book.) So I came naturally to 'making up' people and telling stories about them. I had good examples to follow.

The scripts of my monologues were only written down after days and sometimes weeks of improvising out loud. I made notes of promising lines as I heard myself say them, but only after the voice was established (the key to the whole thing), and the character had taken shape, did I work on the plot; and when these things fused together I committed the whole to paper as a finished draft. Truth to tell, it never was *quite* finished. Performing brought out new ways of speaking and timing lines. I made cuts, altered sequences and occasionally (I didn't often improvise in performance) if a fresh idea surprised me, and I thought it was a good one, I kept it in. But I didn't always remember to alter the original script. Reading through thirty-six years' worth of stage-material to make selections for this small book, I realised how much the monologues had changed since they were first written down. To my amazement I found I could still remember most of the 'new' lines that I had added down the years. The versions here are as I finally played them (I think).

Sometimes in interviews I am asked in which of the media I most enjoyed working. Answer: on stage, live, face to face with an audience, particularly when between us we made instant communication. But the medium for which I most enjoyed writing was radio, because it is the least limiting and calls more than any other on imagination. Over the air it is possible for a large mature woman (like me) to suggest by voice alone that she is slight, probably blonde, green as grass and not more than seventeen.

She can also (or so I hope) conjure up the image of an old Mrs-Noah-shaped Buckin'amshire villager with a face like a crumpled bun. Both these characters are included in this book.

My hope is that as you read you will invent and hear for yourself the sounds each character makes. In reading a monologue, as in hearing it in a theatre or on radio, half the work needed to complete the performance comes from the reader/audience. It is a joint exercise for two imaginations, yours and mine, meeting and making a whole.

None of the lyrics in this collection is really complete without its music, and because I know how much Richard Addinsell's music adds to my words I miss it badly. Please try to imagine (yet again) for yourself delightful, pretty, moving, strong or witty tunes to suit each number. Some tell a story, some are portraits. 'Any Messages, Mrs Bolster?' was written to be read and was never performed. The only lyric in this collection not set by Dick is 'Rainbow Nights', and it was Geoffrey Wright who composed the music for that. 'I'm Going to See You Today' is one of the first songs Dick and I wrote together, during the war in 1942. It is a song in celebration of lovers meeting again after separation. Thirty-six years after we wrote it my recording of it was used to top-and-tail a series of readings from *Joyce Grenfell Requests the*

Pleasure that I did for the BBC. Because many people wrote to say the song celebrated for them joy in their own reunions today (and because I have great affection for it) I include the lyric here.

Dear Reader (as Victorian novelists used to write), I hope you will enjoy contributing your share of imagination in supplying the voices and tunes that go with the words in this book, and may the sum total give you pleasure.

Joyce Grenfell

is pretty isn't it? – and I am going to tell you how to make one just like it. First of all you must obtain some empty beech-nut husk clusters. These are to be found beneath beech trees almost any time about the end of September or October – any time you like – and then wire them on to stalks or stems. (You will find six or eight are ample for a boutonnière.) Now, before you colour you must decide what flower it is you are making. Mine are wood anemones – shell-pink without, and a deeper rose within. (Sometimes I like to use just a suspicion

❧ Useful and Acceptable Gifts ❦

This is the first monologue I ever wrote and performed, on my first stage appearance at the Little Theatre, Adelphi, in Herbert Farjeon's 'Little Revue'. The scene is a village hall in the Southern Counties where the monthly Women's Institute meeting is taking place. The date is probably in October, since the visiting lecturer is being helpful about 'gifts', and Christmas lies ahead.

Madam President, Fellow Institute Members, good evening. This evening I am going to tell you a little bit about my useful and acceptable gifts, and these gifts are not only easy to make but ever so easy to dispose of. I see several of you ladies have your eye on the boutonnière in my lapel – it *is* pretty, isn't it? – and I am going to tell you how to make one just like it. First of all you must obtain some empty beech-nut husk clusters. These are to be found beneath beech trees almost any time after about the middle of September onwards. Cleanse your husks thoroughly. And then wire them on to stalks or stems. (You will find six or eight are ample for a boutonnière.) Now, before you *colour* you must decide what flower it is you are making. Mine are wood anemones – shell-pink without, and a deeper rose within. (Sometimes I like to use just a *suspicion* of gold or silver! I like to feel that we take Nature's gifts and make them even lovelier.) Now, when you are making beech-nut husk flowers do not confine yourself to boutonnières. *Be bold* about it! You can make great sprays of lupes, or delphs.

(If anybody wants to take notes I shan't mind a bit.)

Well, next we come to a more serious gift – waste-paper baskets, or should I say more accurately – waste-paper basket tins, for they are made from manufacturers' biscuit tins, and in order to obtain these you must make love to your grocer and wheedle him into giving one to you. First, cleanse your tin thoroughly and then remove all existing advertising matter. In order to obtain my unusual mosaic design you are going to want some pieces of wallpaper patterns. (I prefer beige tones myself.) Tear your paper up into scraps – the smaller the better – and then paste the pieces all over the *outside* of the tin – higgledy-piggledy, in what you might call a crazy-paving design; and when the pieces are quite firm, outline them in black Indian ink, and you will find you have not only a useful waste-paper basket, but a very unusual piece of modernistic furniture as well.

So much for tins. And lastly we come to what I like to call my comic turn! Dicky Calendars – Dicky Calendars. Dicky is made from two india-rubbers, or, as we called them when I went to school, bunjies! You will want a small one for the head and a strong sturdy one for the body. The head must be joined *to* the body, so obtain some strong wire and pass it through the head and right through poor Dicky's body to emerge as his legs. Mount him on a card-board paper stand, give him two bright pin eyes and a pheasant or chicken's feather for a tail, and then, with a calendar on a jaunty ribbon round his neck, Dicky is ready to keep you up to date!

Ladies, it is our duty as women to beautify our surroundings. Now when you get home I want you to seek out materials to make yourself Useful and Acceptable Gifts. Good evening.

Oh Mr Du Maurier!

I have stood for Mr Millais, and I've sat for
    Madox Brown;
I've been graceful for D. G. Rossetti, in a
    florissy-Morrisy gown.
I seem to delight each pre-Raphaelite, Mr
    Holman Hunt takes me to lunch;
I've been done in half-tones by Sir Edward
    Burne-Jones, but
I've never appeared in *Punch*.

Oh, Mr Du Maurier! Why cannot I be
One of your wittier women like the lady on
    page two three?
There may be prettier women, *plus grande dame*
    maybe;
But they couldn't find one more Du Maurier, or
    more drawrier than me.

The Rossettis read me poems at the house in
  Cheyne Walk;
And Lord Tennyson flattered me lately, in a
  Lordly-Maudly talk.
I seem to incite the writers to write, Mr Ruskin
  admires my mind;
Mr Browning finds I'm like a mystical rhyme,
  Du Maurier only is blind.

Oh, Mr Du Maurier! I would like to know
On what your neglect of me hinges, for it hurts
  my vanity so.
I've got the face and the fringes, so I say,
  pianissimo,
I would sit for you, dear Du Maurier, *con
  amorier molto.*

Oh, Mr Du Maurier! Perhaps I'm out of date.
Time flies when one isn't counting at a beastly
  Priestley rate.
The years must have gone on mounting, and
  now, I estimate
That I'm seventy years, dear Du Maurier, what a
  bore-ier too late.

MOTHERS

Also written for the 'Little Revue'. All the mothers are in their middle thirties. The American comes from the Mid-West; the Understanding Mother is from the Chelsea-Kensington border; and the second of the three is a native of Bucks, where words like 'a little girl' become 'a littoo gurw'. The face I used for this character came as a result of wondering, as I looked at myself in a looking-glass, what would happen, not only to my face but also to my speech, if I put my tongue in front of my lower teeth and spoke. (Try it and see.) That's the face and the sound I used later for another Bucks villager in 'A Terrible Worrier'.

Now, Muriel dear, Mother doesn't want to see that face. We're going to learn this little pome for

Grandma's birthday, and I don't want to hear any more nonsense. I want you to start right from the beginning, after Mother; that is the way to learn. 'Hail to thee, blithe spirit, Bird thou never wert'.

Come on, Muriel, dear, 'Hail . . . Hail to thee blithe spirit'.

What does blithe mean? Blithe means happy spirit – spirit full of joy and happiness. 'Hail to thee, *blithe* spirit, Bird thou never wert'.

I don't know what it was, dear, if it wert not a bird. No, it is not a silly pome, Muriel; it's a very beautiful pome. And Muriel, we don't learn poitry only because it is beautiful but because it teaches us to speak beautifully. You're going to find that very useful later on in life.

It is called 'To a Skylark' by Percy Bysshe Shelley.

Bysshe doesn't mean a thing, dear, it's his name. His mother was probably a Miss Bysshe.

Come on, dear, we aren't getting any place at all; and Muriel, stick in your stomach. Now let's start right from the beginning, after mother. 'To a skylark' – Yes – by Percy – go on – Bysshe – Muriel! Where did you learn that word?

You go right upstairs and wash out your mouth at once!

Ernie, you thank Mrs Tucker for giving you that beautiful lollipop. Oh, he's better now, Mrs Tucker, but he did give us a turn last week. Tuesday it was, about dinner-time. He come in from school, got his head all on the one side. I said to his Dad, don't you think Ernie is a funny colour? His Dad said he did. That was Tuesday. Wednesday he was still like this. I couldn't make it out. We was having a lovely piece of knuckle for dinner, but he couldn't touch it. Just sips of tea, sips of tea. I said to his Dad, 'Look, if he's no better by tomorrow morning you've got go get your bike out and go get the doctor to him.' But it was raining on Thursday. Friday, he was still like this. I tucked him up in bed and give him a hot-water-bottle between his neck and his shoulder; but I couldn't get him a bit comfy. I was just going down the garden to get my bike out to go get the doctor to him when he gives a yell – 'Mum,' he says, 'Mum!' I go upstairs; he's been having a choke. Cough, cough, cough. I thought he was going. All at once up comes a conker! Been lodged in his neck all that time. Oh, he was relieved. Wasn't you, duckie. And do you know why? Because it was a conker he'd borrowed.

Harriet – Harriet, darling – in bed already? Good, because I want to talk to you, darling. I want to talk to you very frankly. Now, I'm not an interfering mother, and I hope I never shall be. This is your life, and you've got to do what you want with it.

All Daddy and I want is your happiness. That's all we want. You see, darling, growing up – well, being grown-up, then – is a very trying time. Don't think I don't know because I do. I know exactly. So does Daddy. We both know exactly. Harriet, I'm afraid you think the reason we don't like Leon is because Leon is a conjuror. Darling, that's not the point at all. It's marvellous to be a conjuror. Daddy says he can't think how he does it. But have you considered what it would be like to be a conjuror's wife? Do you think you could stand it? I know I couldn't. Rabbits popping in and out of things all the time. And it seems to me *that* is your problem. Do you think you could be really happy married to a middle-aged Portuguese conjuror? No, darling, we won't discuss it any more tonight because I want you to sleep well and look pretty tomorrow morning. And darling, I'm not in the least worried about you. Nor is Daddy. There is *nothing* to be worried about. I'm not in the *least* worried.

Dear François
Out of the blue I write to you to say that all is
well in London still. I trust your wife is well? –
You too? Do write and tell me all your news. My
daughter, Adrienne, is growing up. She's seventeen
today. I thought you'd like to know – after so long
– that all is well here.

I wish you could see my daughter,
She's not in the least like me.
She's small and dark and lightly made,
Not in the least bit English, I'm afraid.
I wish you could see my daughter,
She's amusing and she's kind.
She's got a lively mind, like you.
I'm very proud of her.

There's no excuse for writing now,
I thought I never would.
What's past is past,
And both of us are happy now,
And so the news is good.
Perhaps I'm wrong in writing,
But the war's so far away –
Another world,
But I am grateful for the past today.

I wish you could know my daughter,
Oh, I'm prejudiced, I agree,
But none the less she does impress
Everyone else, and so it's not just me.
I felt I must talk about her,
But it's the middle of the night,
And a foolish time to write.
I said I never would.

Dear François,
Have no fear, I will not fail.
This letter will not reach you,
That I swear.
I write you every year,
But none of my letters
Ever catch the mail.

Thought for Today

For the original, English version of this sketch, written in 1950 for 'Penny Plain', the speaker used the same bright South-of-England suburban voice as the W.I. lecturer in 'Useful and Acceptable Gifts'. When I went to Broadway for the first time in 1954 I re-wrote the monologue and changed the background and income group of the enthusiastic speaker. This American woman has houses on Long Island and in Maine, a farm in Virginia and an apartment (or maybe a duplex?) in Manhattan, the scene of the sketch. She frequently crosses the Atlantic. The long drawling vowel sounds I used for this woman once indicated immense wealth. The same vowel sounds are heard in her fluent French.

Lily, darling . . . How divine to see you. Come right on in.

Dimitri, voulez-vous apporter les drinks ici au librairie, toute suite. Oui, toutes les bouteilles. Isn't he divine, Lily? He's the only white Russian butler left in the whole of New York. I found him in Paris and he's so typical. Moody and depressing. Just the way the Russians used to be. So much more fun. But Lily, come and sit down. I can't wait to tell you what's happened to me.

My dear, I am entirely different . . . Well, I am inside.

Lily, have you ever heard of Dr Pelting? My dear, you're going to. He is the most marvellous man in the whole world, and he knows the answer to everything.

Lily, you know how I worried? O, I mean I worried so I fell asleep all the time doing it . . . just talking to people or playing bridge . . . and I worried whether to go to California or get my hair cut. And I worried whether it was wrong to be so rich. But Dr Pelting says it isn't in the least wrong. He says it's fine to be rich.

You see he's made this marvellous discovery.

Lily, Dr Pelting's message to you, to me, to the whole world . . . is simply this:

Don't think.

Isn't it *exciting*? O, I know what you're going to

say. What will happen if I don't think? And the marvellous answer is . . . Nothing! Because Earth Ray Thought Forces are going to think for you. It seems the earth is full of wonderful forces, but how to make contact?

Lily, where do we touch the earth most closely? Exactly . . . our feet. And what we get through our feet are Earth Ray Thought Forces.

I met him at Emily's. I'd had my face done, so I thought I might as well use it, and I put on a new little black dress I got at Balmain and some divine perfume called *Fiasco*, and honestly I didn't feel too unattractive. But this man came over to me, and he said 'You need help', and I said 'How do you *know*?' and he told me he had been guided to me by Earth Ray Thought Forces. And he told me that these forces enter the body through the soles of the feet, and that's the way they influence the mind. And he said anybody can renew supplies if they will only stand in earth night and morning, if possible facing north.

I said to him, 'Look, sweetie, I can do that out in the country down at the farm in Virginia, but I cannot do it here in New York, on the eighteenth floor. And anyway I don't know which way north is.'

But he said, 'Look, all you have to do is get yourself a little tray, fill it with earth and stand in that.' And, he said, any passing Girl Scout will tell you which way north is.

He is a man of such vision.

Well, we went to the country that weekend, and I stood in earth every day, night and morning, even when it rained. I did it in a flower-bed, and it certainly felt as if I was facing north.

Well, when I'd gotten over a silly little chest cold I came back to New York, and I got myself a little tray, and I use it all the time. Walthrop says he doesn't know me any more. I tried to make him do it too, but you know he is so blind to his basic needs, and he says he gets all he wants in life from Benzedrine.

But I couldn't do without E.R.T.F. – Earth Ray Thought Force; and Eddie – Dr Pelting – comes in here on his way home sometimes, and we do it together on my little tray. Well, because two people make twice as much force.

No, he's not good-looking. He's . . . . he's just very vital.

Lily, you must try it. You'll love it. Let's go find my little tray right now.

O merci, Dimitri . . . mettez les drinks ici, là, sur le piano. O bon. Little cheesy things. *Merci. Non, c'est tout. Merci.*

You know, Lily, he's not as gloomy as he used to be. I wonder if he's been using my little tray . . . ?

The Countess of Coteley

The Countess of Coteley!
Wife of the Eleventh Earl,
Mother of four fine children,
Three boys and a girl.
Coteley Park in Sussex,
Strathrar on the Dee,
Palace Gardens, Kensington,
Aged thirty-three.

Look at the Countess of Coteley!
Here you see her when
She was at her zenith and the year
was nineteen-ten.

Is she happy, would you guess?
The answer to that question is, more or less.

For she's never heard of Hitler, and she's never
    thought of war,
She's got twenty-seven servants, and she could
    get twenty more.
She never sees a paper, and she seldom reads a
    book,
She is worshipped by her butler, tolerated by her
    cook.
And her husband treats her nicely, and he's
    mostly on a horse,
While the children are entirely in the nursery of
    course.
So no wonder she is happy – she's got nothing
    else to do.
O, no wonder she is happy, for she hasn't got a clue,
To the future that is waiting, and the funny
    things she'll do
About . . . thirty-seven years from now.

When you see her in this flashback it is rather
    hard to guess
That she'll be a sort of typist in the W.V.S.
She will learn to woo her grocer: she won't have
    a cook to woo,
But a Czechoslovak cleaner may pop in from
    twelve to two.
Speaking worldlily she'll dwindle. She will
    change her book at Boots,

And lecture on Make-do-and-Mend to Women's
Institutes.
She will lose the Earl quite quietly, and her young
will leave the nest,
She never knew them very well, so that is for the
best.
And Coteley, Strathrar, Kensington will vanish
with the rest
About . . . thirty-seven years from now.

Now the National Trust has Coteley, which is
quite a handy dodge,
And she'll make a flat of part of what was once
the keeper's lodge.
She will seldom dress for dinner, she will dote
on Vera Lynn,
She will take in the *New Statesman*, but she won't
be taken in.

Here you see her in this flashback looking
decorative but dumb,
For she hasn't got an inkling of the jolly days to
come!
Though the distances she'll travel are incredible
to tell,
And the quandaries she'll cope with will be
absolutely hell,
She'll emerge in Forty-seven having done it
rather well!

Will she be happy, would you guess?
The answer to that question is . . . Y-e-s.

Life and Literature

A young girl sits at the feet of a successful novelist.

I feel as if I'd known you for absolute ages instead
of only half an hour. It was awfully clever of you
to find such a lovely quiet place, even if it is a bit
dark. Of course, in a way I do know you through
your books, and when Alison said 'Do come in on
Friday because Lionel Pilgrim is going to be there,'
I almost died. I said 'Not *the* Lionel Pilgrim?' and
she said 'Yes.' I almost died.

Yes, I've read all your books. No, I haven't got
them. I got them out of the library. They didn't
actually have them, but they got them for me. Well,
I think it's your honesty I admire so much. You
know, the way you use rude words and that. And
then you always have such original backgrounds.

I never knew Edinburgh was like that. Oh, I've been through it on the way to places, but you know, it didn't seem like that.

Oh, I know what I thought was absolutely *marvellous*. You know that man in the book you wrote about Istanbul – *Sin is a Fair Flower* – well, I thought it was so marvellous the way you made him so harsh and evil, and so cruel to his wife – branding her and everything – and yet all the time, deep down, he was frightfully religious. I was awfully surprised when he became a nun – I mean a monk.

I say, you had a very unhappy childhood, didn't you? Oh, I just guessed. Well, you are Henry in *The Heart has no Womb*, aren't you? I thought so. Poor you. It must have been awful. I mean about your father, and then having to be a Wolf Cub when you couldn't believe in it. You know that bit in the disused gravel-pit where the girl taunted you? Well, I don't think, I *absolutely* understood it quite, though I thought it was awfully interesting. Frightfully clever.

Oh, I had a very happy childhood. Well, we lived in the country and I had a pony . . . and lots of cousins . . . and we played games, and had fun . . . and I used to scribble a bit. Poetry. I still do, actually. Oh no, it's no good at all. Absolutely hopeless. Well, Mummy thinks it's quite good, but

I mean it *isn't*. Oh no, not love poems, more things like Spring, and Flowers . . . and Death.

My hair isn't in the least bit Greek! I just twist it up and it stays there. No, I couldn't possibly take it down. Because I should feel so frightfully silly. No, I couldn't possibly. I say, are you feeling hungry? I mean, we could go back to the buffet or something. No, I'm not in the least hungry. I love just sitting here and talking.

Don't be silly, my skin, isn't in the least transparent.

Do shut up.

I say, may I ask you something? Well, do you think that if a person is going to write about the sort of things you write about, do they have to actually experience all those things before they can write about them?

Oh. – Well then, I don't suppose I'll ever write *anything*. Well, I live in the country, and absolutely *nothing* ever happens . . .

Oh, I'd love to come and have dinner with you one evening and talk about it. What fun!

May I bring Mummy?

Stately as a Galleon

My neighbour, Mrs Fanshaw, is portly-plump
  and gay,
She must be over sixty-seven, if she is a day.
You might have thought her life was dull,
It's one long whirl instead.
I asked her all about it, and this is what she
  said:

I've joined an Olde Thyme Dance Club, the
  trouble is that there
Are too many ladies over, and no gentlemen to
  spare.
It seems a shame, it's not the same,
But still it has to be,
Some ladies have to dance together,
One of them is me.

Stately as a galleon, I sail across the floor,
Doing the Military Two-step, as in the days of
  yore.
I dance with Mrs Tiverton; she's light on her
  feet, in spite
Of turning the scale at fourteen stone, and
  being of medium height.
So gay the band,
So giddy the sight,
Full evening dress is a must,
But the zest goes out of a beautiful waltz
When you dance it bust to bust.

So, stately as two galleons, we sail across the
  floor,
Doing the Valse Valeta as in the days of yore.
The gent is Mrs Tiverton, I am her lady fair,
She bows to me ever so nicely and I curtsey to
  her with care.
So gay the band,
So giddy the sight,
But it's not the same in the end
For a lady is never a gentleman, though
She may be your bosom friend.

So, stately as a galleon, I sail across the floor,
Doing the dear old Lancers, as in the days of
  yore.

I'm led by Mrs Tiverton, she swings me round
and round
And though she manoeuvres me wonderfully
well
I never get off the ground.

So gay the band,
So giddy the sight,
I try not to get depressed.
And it's done me a power of good to explode,
And get this lot off my chest.

Shirley's Girl Friend

The series of 'Shirl' scripts originated on radio at the end of the war, and I wrote a great many sketches for this South London girl in conversation with her friend, Shirl. Some were written for performance on stage, and when Benjamin Britten invited me to be part of the festival at Aldeburgh in Suffolk in 1964 (the highest honour I ever received), I wrote this Shirl for the occasion.

Shirl, you ever been to a Musical Festival?

Well, you know my boy, Norm – the one drives the lorry with the big ears. Well, him and me got all involved in a Musical Festival last summer, all unbeknownst. Well, Norm's got this friend, Walter, who's a musician. He's a *professional* musician. I mean, he can do it even when he's not in the mood. He's on clarionet – by trade that is – but on the side he's got up this group. They're all record players. They play on the recorder.

Yes, I know it's kid stuff, the recorder. They done it when I was at school, but this Walham Green Recorder Consort Group is different because they only do unusual music. 'Little known rarities', he was telling me. *Very* old music. They was dances mostly, galliards and that, and they got very old names like 'Lord Partelotte's Reluctance' and 'Catch Jenny Bending'. It's like old time Olde Tyme Dancing.

Oh, they do Modern Contemporary, too. They've had a piece specially wrote for them by a Frenchman, called 'Experience from A to B'. It's all on just the two notes, he was telling me. Very clever, you know.

Well, this Walter come over to Norm's Mum's the other Sunday on his way home from a practice, see, and he hears me do me whistlin'. Because I whistle all right. You know I won a talent contest doin' me whistlin' once, whistlin' the Sabre Dance (*whistles it*) by – by – oh, wait a minute. I used to have a clever way of rememberin' his name. *I* know:

Catcha choo-choo-train. That's it. Katcha-churian. Well this Walter likes the way I whistle, see, and he gets all excited and he says to me:

'Can you read music?'

I said: 'Not so's you'd notice it.'

'Oh,' he says, 'you are deprived.'

'Well,' I said, 'I never felt the need of it. If I like a tune I can pick it up.'

And Norm says, 'You never know where it's been though, do you?'

So we all has a laugh, and then this Walter says: 'You whistle damn well.'

'Don't mention,' I says, 'it's just a gift from the gods.'

'No,' he says, 'you do. If only you could read the dots like any other fulfilled adult you'd come in useful to me.'

'Who?' I says, 'Me?'

'Yes,' he says. And he tells me this Walham Green Recorder Consort's been asked to go to the East Marshmere Festival of Music and the Arts to perform a very Elizabethan rarity called 'Friar Balsam's Repeat'. And it's got like this whistlin' echo part in it has to be done by the human whistle. And Walter says his regular whistler can't do it no more because he's had a tooth out. 'Do you think,' he says, 'you could learn the echo part in "Friar Balsam's Repeat" and do it at the Festival with us on the twenty-fourth?'

'Why not?' I says. 'I might as well live danger-ously while I still got all me choppers. Come on, Walt, when do we start? What's wrong with now?' So I learn it. It's not difficult, you see. They do it first, and then I just echo it. And it's nice and slow. I like slow music – because it's more musical.

Well, I practise and practise on me own *and* I go once a week to the boys at Walham Green. And on the evening before the concert Walter says to me: 'What are you going to wear?' He says: 'Now *don't* wear nothing too swinging and with it, will you? And *don't* have your hair backcombed up so bouffant nobody can't see past you. And *don't* wear your tangerine blouse with your petunia purple two-piece, because none of them things looks right in a thirteenth-century church.'

'Finished?' I said.

'Yes,' he says.

'Oh,' I says. 'So it's in a church is it, then of *course* I shall wear me skin-tight tiger-skin drainpipes and a bikini top – *if* it's in a church.' I says to him: 'Whom do you think I am that I don't know what's what to wear on such and such an occasion! I am going to wear a very simple, snow-white, uncluttered, up-and-down shift.'

Norm says: 'Don't overdo it. I mean pure's pure, but you only got the one whistling echo. Don't take off or anything, will yer?'

'Look,' I says, 'if a thing's worth doing well it's worth doing at all. "Friar Balsam's Repeat" is seldom heard today and it's got to be good in sound and sight.'

So I wore me up-and-down shift. But I needn't of bothered, because I was stood behind the pulpit, so I would sound more like a distant echo. Nobody saw a living inch of me. I might as well of kept on me plastic mac. Still, the concert was a big success. They don't applaud in church, you know, but you can tell when they like it. They breathe heavy.

And Walter was pleased with me. He said all my intonations was dead on every time. I'm not sure what it means but I think he meant it nicely. Norm says it was all right from where he was, out in the graveyard. Because he couldn't come inside, it made him nervous knowing I was goin' to do me whistlin'.

He said: 'D'you know what it sounded like?'

So I says: 'No?'

'It was just like a girl trying to whistle like she was a far away echo.'

He's a great comfort to me that Norm.

Oh, he is nice.

Learn to Loosen

On the back of a literary weekly
Under 'Personal' I read it, just by chance.
It was meant for me to see, 'twas intended it
    should be,
Or I thought so from that first haphazard
    glance.
'Yours,' it said, 'the rhythms of the earth and
    sea and sky.'
'Learn,' it said, 'to dance the natural nature way.
Let the music through, find the inner you.
Two minutes' walk from Paddington Station,
    join our group today.'

So I went then and there and enrolled
And this is what I was told:
'Learn to loosen, loosen, loosen, loosen,

Bend to the music, just give way.
Go with the music where it takes you,
Don't be afraid if it leads you astray.
Listen to the music, get its message,
Learn to hear what the music will say,
Listen, listen, listen, listen,
Hark to the music and dance away.'

I stood where I was and relaxed as I should
I waited and waited the message to hear.
I listened and listened, but hark as I would
The music said only one thing in my ear:
'You're a horse,' said the music, 'a great white
    horse
And you gallop and gallop and gallop the
    course,
And you leap and you leap and you whinney
    and neigh,
And you gallop and gallop and gallop away.'

'Rest,' said the teacher, 'Now listen anew.
You must learn to loosen or nothing comes
    through.'
So 'Loosen, loosen, loosen, loosen,
Bend to the music, just give way.
Go with the music where it takes you
Don't be afraid if it leads you astray.
Listen to the music, get its message,

Learn to hear what the music will say,
Listen, listen, listen, listen,
Hark to the music and dance away.'

'Rest,' said the teacher, 'Now listen my dear,
What is the musical message you hear?'
'You're *still* a horse,' said the music, 'a great
white horse,
And you gallop and gallop and gallop the
course,
And you leap and you leap and you whinney
and neigh,
And you gallop and gallop and gallop away.'

Visitor

I am never quite certain whether this speaker is Dutch or Scandinavian; possibly Dutch with a Scandinavian mother. She, too, travels a great deal with her high-powered businessman husband. The scene is yet another crowded cocktail party, where, of course, there is nowhere to sit. (For the American season in 1955 I wrote an American version of this sketch.)

Is dis not a smeshing cocktail party? I am so fond for a cocktail party. I sink is so nice to say hello and goodbye quick, and to have little sings for eating is so gay. Is always quite noisy and nowhere for sitting.

Yes, ve are here in London vis my husband. My husband is having business associate here in London, so ve are coming to London – and to Oslo, Copenhagen, Amsterdam, Paris, London – all over; and everyvere dere is a cocktail party. Most kind.

You are knowing Lady Hetting? She is a tall, sin Englis lady, and ven I am here two year ago Lady Hetting is most kind for me. Ve are making a sight-see together. O ve are seeing Piccadiddly, and ve are seeing some modern art works at de Tate Gallery and ve are going to de Ideal Homes Exhibition. Lady Hetting is good for cooking. I am for bringing her a little gift horse. Is a chipple chopper. A chipple chopper? O dis is a little gedget knife for cutting up celery. I sink she vill find him most useless.

Hello, how are you? I am smeshing vell senk you. You have see Lady Hetting? No, not yet. Tata just now.

Senk you, I would like somesing for eating. Vat is det? No senk you.

You are from London? Oh, you are from Cardiff. Det is nice. I was once in Scotland.

Senk you? Oh, I would like somesing for eating. Vat is det? No senk you.

Oh Mrs Antrobus! I am so happy for seeing you again. May I present here is a nice gentleman from Scotland. Dis is Mrs Antrobus from God-alming in Surrey. How is Mr Antrobus? And you are still heving det little cat? You know ve are always laughing and talking about dis little cat from Mr and Mrs Antrobus. Is a most intelligent amusing little animal. You remember your little cat? Oh, I sought it was you was heving det little cat? Are you sure? A little cat vis a vite under? Vell it vas dis little cat was sneezing in rhythm to de music of Brahms. He is not sneezing for Mozart, not for Beethoven, Shostakovich, Chopin. No, no, only Brahms, and ven you vas going to de piano dis little cat vas for sneezing. Oh, you have no piano and no little cat? Oh, so sad.

I sink it vas a little cat from London, but ve are many places all over – ve are in Buenos Aires, in Melbourne, in Slough, all over. Ve are always somevere. So tiring.

Hello, how are *you*? I am sensational, senk you. No, I do not yet see Lady Hetting. I sink she is not coming. She is here? Vere? O dere, in de doorvay in de purple dress vis die Mexican jewelry. Hoo, hoo. O I am *so* heppy for seeing your jolly old face again.

Yes, ve vould like somesing for eating. Vat is dose? Senk you. I vill try . . .

Is dere an ashtray?

At the Laundrette

They have chamber music concerts at the Town
  Hall,
At the library you can read and read and read,
There are churches and a chapel,
And societies where they grapple with *all* sorts
  of problems
But they none of them met our need.
We were hungry for some wider sort of experi-
  ence,
We were restless and as nervy as could be,
Then we all of a sudden found fulfilment,
And we found it where you wouldn't of thought
  it would be.

We found fulfilment at the Laundrette,
Life took on a meaning rich and new.

It's impossible to think when you're standing at
    the sink,
But down at the Laundrette there is nothing else
    to do.
You can think or you can read or you can natter –
It doesn't really matter what you do –
And it's such a loverly treat,
Not to be standing on your feet
At the Laundrette, the loverly Laundrette,
Oh, we've found fulfilment at the Laundrette.

Glad, here, is absolutely altered –
Mondays were her misery before.
She would start the day with dread,
Seeing agony ahead,
But now with the Laundrette she's not worried
    any more.
She is calm and she is cool and she is grateful,
Her Mondays are not hateful any more,
She is just a shining ray,
Every minute of the day.

Neither Glad nor me, we
Don't go to the pub, see,
We like it more at the Laundrette
And use it more like a club.
It's ever so peaceful and clean there,
It does you good to be seen there,

You never know who is next to you,
And you never know who's just been there,
Washing the towels and shirts and sheets,
And socks and frocks, etcetera,
Used to get worse and worser and worser,
But now it gets betterer and betterer.

We found fulfilment at the Laundrette,
We've found a wider purpose in our lives.
We have made a little clique,
And we meet there in the week,
And all through the Laundrette we're becoming
    better wives.
In these ugly days when everyone is greedy,
We were needy for a sunbeam in our lives.
And the sunbeam we have found,
As our washing whizzes round,
Is the Laundrette,
The loverly Laundrette,
We've found fulfilment at the Laundrette.

Committee

The ladies are assembled in Mrs Hailestone's front room somewhere north of Birmingham. The telly is full on. It is time to start the meeting.

Well, let's get down to business, shall we?

Would you be so good as to turn off your telly, please, Mrs Hailestone? Thank you. That's better. It's very good of you to let us use your front room. I think we're all assembled. Mrs Brill, Miss Culch, Mrs Pell, Mrs Hailestone, May and me. All right then, May, let's have the minutes of the last meeting.

Oh, May. You're supposed to have them in that little book I gave you. I told you last time. You're supposed to write down everything we do and say and then read it out at the next meeting, and I sign it.

I know we all know what we said and did, dear, but you have to write it down. That's what minutes are for.

Don't cry, May, dear. Let's get on with the next item on the agenda. Apologies for Absence. You read out the excuses. Oh, May. Well, you must try and remember to bring your glasses next time. All right, I'll read them. Give them here. Cheer up.

Mrs Slope is very sorry she's caught up. Can't come.

Miss Heddle's got her mother again. Can't come.

Lady Widmore sent a telegram 'ALAS CANNOT BE WITH YOU DEVASTATED'. Can't come.

Well then. As you all know, this is *another* special meeting of the Ladies' Choral to talk about the forthcoming Festival and County Choral Competition. We know the date and we know the set song. Yes we do, May. It's in two parts for ladies' voices in E flat, 'My Bosom is a Nest'.

But of course what we are really here for tonight is this very important question of voices in the choir. Now, we don't want any unpleasantness. Friendly is what we are, and friendly is how we are going to go on. But it's no good beating about the bush, we all know there is *one* voice among the altos that did not ought to be there. And I think we all know to what I am referring.

Now, don't think that I don't like Mrs Codlin, because I do. Yes, she *is* a very nice woman. Look at how nice she is with her little car – giving us all lifts here and there. And she's a lovely lender – lends you her books, and her knitting patterns, recipes, anything. Lovely. Yes, she is a regular churchgoer *and* a most generous donator to the fund. But she just has this one fault: she does not blend.

May, dear, would you be so kind as to slip out and see if I left the lamp turned off on my bike? I don't want to waste the battery, and I can't remember if I did it. Thank you, May.

Ladies, I didn't like to say anything in front of May, but I must remind you that Mrs Codlin's voice is worse than what ever May's was; and you know what happened the last time we let May sing in the competition. We were disqualified. So you see it is very important and very serious.

Oh thank you, May, dear. Had I? I am a big silly, aren't I?

You see, it isn't as if Mrs Codlin had a voice you could ignore. I mean you can't drown her out. They can hear her all down the road, over the sopranos; yes, over your piano, Mrs Pell, over everything. You know, I was stood next to her at practice last week when we did 'The Wild Brown Bee is my Lover'. When we'd finished I said to her very tactfully, thinking she might like to take the hint, I said: 'I wonder who it is stands out so among the altos?' and she said she hadn't noticed. Hadn't noticed! Mrs Brill was on her other side and she said to me afterwards, didn't you, Mrs Brill? she said the vibrations were so considerable they made her chest hum.

No, I know she doesn't do it on purpose, May.

No, of course she didn't ought to have been let in in the first place. It's ridiculous. It makes a nonsense of music. But the thing is, it was her idea, wasn't it? She founded the choir.

Do you think if anyone was to ask her very nicely not to sing it might stop her? I mean we could let her come and just stand there. Yes, Mrs Hailestone, she does *look* like a singer, I'll give her that. That's the annoying part.

Would anybody like to ask her? Well, has anybody got any suggestions?

No, May, not anonymous letters. They aren't very nice.

May . . . ?

I wonder . . . May, one of your jobs as secretary is watching the handbags and the coats at competitions, isn't it? I mean you have to stay in the cloakroom all during the competitions, don't you? I thought so. Look, May; now don't think we don't appreciate you as secretary – we do, dear, don't we ladies? – But would you like to resign? Just say yes now, and I'll explain it all later. Lovely.

Well, we accept your resignation, and I would like to propose that we appoint Mrs Codlin secretary and handbag-watcher for the next competition. Anybody second that? Thank you, Mrs Hailestone. Any against? Then that's passed unanimously. Lovely. Oh, I know it's not in order, Mrs Pell, but we haven't any minutes to prove it. May didn't have a pencil, did you, May?

Well, I think it's a very happy solution. We get rid of her and keep her at one and the same time.

What did you say, May? Can *you* sing if Mrs Codlin doesn't?

Oh, May, you've put us right back to square one.

Three Brothers

I had Three Brothers,
Harold and Robert and James,
All of them tall and handsome,
All of them good at games.
And I was allowed to field for them,
To bowl to them, to score:
I was allowed to slave for them
For ever and evermore.
Oh, I was allowed to fetch and carry for my
    Three Brothers,
Jim and Bob and Harry.

All of my brothers,
Harry and Jim and Bob,
Grew to be good and clever,
Each of them at his job.

135

And I was allowed to wait on them,
To be their slave complete,
I was allowed to work for them
And life for me was sweet,
For I was allowed to fetch and carry for my
    Three Brothers,
Jim and Bob and Harry.

Jim went out to South Africa,
Bob went out to Ceylon,
Harry went out to New Zealand
And settled in Wellington.
And the grass grew high on the cricket-pitch,
And the tennis-court went to hay,
And the place was too big and too silent
After they went away.

So I turned it into a Guest House,
After our parents died,
And I wrote to the boys every Sunday,
And once a year they replied.
All of them married eventually,
I wrote to their wives, of course,
And their wives wrote back on postcards –
Well . . . it might have been very much worse.

And now I have nine nieces,
Most of them home at school.

I have them all to stay here
For the holidays, as a rule.

And I am allowed to slave for them,
To do odd jobs galore,
I am allowed to work for them
And life is sweet once more,
For I am allowed to fetch and carry for the chil-
    dren of
Jim and Bob and Harry.

LALLY TULLETT

In her rocking-chair reading a local newspaper is an old woman. It is a hot summer-night and she and an old friend, Charlotte, are out on the porch of her house in Virginia.

Lord have mercy, Charlotte, guess who's dead? Lally Tullett! Lally Tullett. Remember? You knew her din't yer? I thought you knew her! Taught school here. It was just after Dan and I moved here, I guess. Maybe it was before you and Andrew came. I know it was a long time ago. I think my children were only little then and Fanny had just started school and John was home and I think I must have been carrying Tuppy that summer. Yes, I was, and little Dan hadn't even been thought of. Lord, that's a long time ago. Must be fifty-five –

fifty-six years ago. My Lord! (*Reads*) 'Miss Lally Tullett of 1574 Cedar Oaks Avenue, Gainsford, North Carolina' (never knew she came from down there) 'sometime schoolteacher of this city, died Monday.'

Well, well; and Charlotte she was older'n me. I never knew that. She was very . . . not real pretty but kinder interestin' lookin'. Sometimes she was pretty as paint and sometimes plainer'n hell . . . but you had to look at her twice. She had style. She had great big old brown eyes and she was kinder skinny but she had *style*. I remember she had a cream-coloured linen suit with white braid trim on it and a white shirtwaist. I craved that cream-coloured linen suit!

That *was* the summer I was carrying Tuppy and I thought he'd never get here. Lally roomed over at Mrs Hackett's, had that big room out the back, the one that keeps cool in summer, and she brought all her own books and pictures with her when she came. She was a great reader, and she could speak poetry and she was crazy about good music; but there wasn't much of that around here then. I don't remember anybody had a phonograph and the only person who had a pianner was Dr Kinton. He played real good. Crossed his hands and everything. Remember? He went over to Vienna to learn to be a doctor and while he was there he took pianner lessons . . . and when he come home he bought hisself a great big old grand pianner, and whenever he had any time, he'd play that old pianner. He wasn't married then. Summer nights, with all the doors and winders wide open, you could hear him clear up here. Just as well his house was set back some. I think you can have too much good music when it's only practising.

Want some more coffee? Help yourself.

Lally used to saunter up the lane to Dr Kinton's in the summer evenings and sit on the bank outside his house so she could hear him playin'. No, she wouldn't go inside. Oh, he asked her but she wouldn't go. She just wasn't sociable. Everybody asked her to their homes but she wouldn't go . . . and she wouldn't date anybody. They asked her. Oh, they asked her all right. She was young and pretty enough and there wasn't that many pretty girls around, but she wouldn't go.

The only place she ever came was to our house. Well, we're right next to Mrs Hackett's and she used to come and play with the children in the yard. And then she'd come in the house and she and my Dan would argue. Lord, they'd argue about anything; politics and women's rights. She was kind of radical and it riled him. No, I couldn't argue with anybody. I haven't the brains nor the inclination.

I said to Lally one day, 'Lally Tullett, don't you want to get married?'

And she said, 'Yes, Hetty, I do.'

I told her, I said, 'Well, you are certainly going about it in a mighty funny way. All the nice young men round here want to date you and give you a good time but you always say No. You want to watch it or maybe you won't find somebody to love.'

She didn't say nothin'.

I said, 'Lally, have you found somebody? Hell, Lally, who?'

She said, 'I do not want to discuss it.'

She was like that. Brusk. Closer than a clam. Well, sir, I was pretty damn sure she had her eye on Dr Kinton, and I didn't blame her. He was a lovely man, and she wasn't the only one thought so. I thought she was playin' hard to get but I didn't say a word. I decided I'd just sit back and watch it all develop.

Well, sir, it was a mighty hot summer, hotter'n purgatory, and I felt all tuckered out with it; and one Sunday we were invited to a big picnic party over at the Forwells'. 'Member the Forwells had that house where the Presbyterian Church is now? They had more money than sense, and that bow-legged daughter with the red hair. She picked up her skirts in a three-legged race and we all saw! Just as well she had money.

I said to Dan, 'You take the children and have your-selves a good time. I'll just stay here and be quiet.'

He said, 'You sure you're all right, Hetty?'

I said, 'Honey, just leave me be. All I want to do is get my feet off the ground and get towards having this little old baby born.'

So they went off and I went up to my bedroom and I took off my dress. I took off my corset and I put on a thin wrapper and I lay down on my bed. It was the same old four-poster bed I still sleep in. (Used to be Dan's grandmother's but I'm going to give it to my grand-daughter. Because she's crazy for it, thinks it's antique. I don't know where she's goin' to put it in that two-room apartment, but she can have it if she wants it.) I must have slept longer than I thought for when I woke up it was dark and there was a storm going on! You never heard anything like in all your born days. The winders were rattling and the doors banging and the rain was hittin' the winders like stones.

I was startled for a minute and I didn't know where I was. I got up and lit a lamp and closed the winders and fastened the doors. I felt like I'd come from out some long dark tunnel and it was like as if I was the only person in the whole wide world . . . and I was scared, Charlotte.

I remember I was standin' on the corner of the stairway by the old clock, and although the storm was making a terrible noise I could still hear that old clock tickin' . . . tick – tock – tick – tock – tick – tock. A mighty lonesome sound. And my heart was going about twice as fast . . . tick-tock-tick-tock. And then all of a sudden, as if it was written in letters of fire on the wall, I *knew* . . . that Dan and Lally . . . don't ask me how I knew . . . I just knew it, that's all. I just knew. I didn't know what to do. I just stood there and I said, 'Oh, no . . . no . . . oh, no . . .'

And then Dan come home with the children and I made 'em go straight upstairs to bed. I didn't know what I was doin'. I was so shocked. I couldn't be sweet to 'em. I made 'em cry. Well, I got 'em into bed and I came downstairs and I said to Dan, 'What do you want for supper?' And he said he didn't want nothin' but a glass of milk, and I couldn't have forced a crumb between my lips with a hammer and chisel.

We went out on the porch and the storm had moved off some, but you could still hear the rain hittin' on the leaves. I was mightly glad it was dark. We sat there and after a while I said, 'Dan, I want to ask you somp'n. Are you happy?'

And he said, 'Hetty, I want to tell you . . .'

I said, 'Dan, don't you say anything that's going to make it impossible for me and you to get right back where we are now.'

He said, 'Hetty, I just want you to know . . .'

I said, 'I don't *want* to know . . . I don't want to know . . .'

I went upstairs to the bedroom. I closed the door and I went to bed. I couldn't even say me prayers. And Lord, it was hot. It was hotter than Tophet. And I was cold like I was a piece of ice . . .

I don't believe I ever saw Lally again . . . I know she moved away soon after that but I don't remember if I saw her ever again; and I don't think Dan did either. He never mentioned her name to his dying day.

Lordy, that was a long time ago! It was a hundred million years ago . . . I have *not thought* of Lally Tullet in all this long while. Lord have mercy . . .

Mmm! Lally Tullett . . . Mmm.

I certainly did crave that cream-coloured linen suit.

Do you know somp'n, Charlotte?

She never did get married . . .

RAINBOW NIGHTS

At the end of the war there was a canteen called
Rainbow Corner, run for U.S. forces in London,
in Shaftesbury Avenue, just off Piccadilly Circus.
The place was a mecca for London girls, on
Saturday nights in particular. They were drawn
by the bright lights, cheerful decor, plentiful
supply of young men who loved to dance and
were good at it. They also enjoyed sodas, sand-
wiches and flattery of a kind they were not used
to. The scene of this number is a kitchen hung
with nappies. The girls who sing the duet are now
wives and mums and happy; but they can't help
looking back with wistful nostalgia to those
glamorous nights, when they used to 'go up West
to the Corner'.

When we were young, oh, *years* ago,
The Yanks and the Canadians was here.
Me and Gladys had some fun,
Didn't we, Glad?
We did.
Now we're married, happily.
Our boys got back at last.
I married Ken, she married Len,
And both of them is lovely men,
But all the same just now and then
We like to dream of the past.
Me and Gladys had some fun, we did,
Didn't we, Glad?
We did.

Saturday nights at Rainbow Corner!
Me and Glad would go up West
Through the blackout in the winter
Dressed up in our best.
It was lovely, wasn't it, Glad?
'Hiya, Babe!' and 'Hey, Goodlookin'!'
'Come to Poppa!' – 'Say, what's cookin'?'
Hank and Joe and Red and Slim
Standin' on the corner there, chewin',
'Hiya, Gorgeous, how'm I doin'?'
Wasn't it lovely, Glad?
Just to think of it makes you sad.
Wasn't it lovely, Glad?

Lovely times at Rainbow Corner!
All that food and warmth and lights,
Bubblegum and Coca-cola,
All the dancin' through the nights.
It was lovely, wasn't it, Glad?
'Hiya, sweetheart, what a dame!'
'Hiya, honey, what's your name?'
Hank and Joe and Red and Slim
Standin' on the corner there, lazy.
'Hiya, dream girl, let's go crazy.'
Wasn't it lovely, Glad?
Just to think of it makes you sad.
Wasn't it lovely, Glad?

Now we're married girls it's nice
To think back to the days gone by.
We had lovely outin's then,
Didn't we, May?
We did.
We worked in the fact'ry then,
Hard it was and fast,
But then we used to get away,
And then we'd let ourselves go gay
And we was rich on all that pay.
It's nice to dream of the past.
Me and Gladys had some fun, we did.
Didn't we, Glad?
We did.

Saturday nights at Rainbow Corner!
Me and May our hair done swank
On our shoulders soft and silky,
Set for dancin' with a Yank.
It was lovely, wasn't it, Glad?
'Hiya, Baby, hey, Goodlookin'.'
'Come to Poppa!' – 'Say, what's cookin'?'
Hank and Joe and Red and Slim
Leanin' on the corner there winkin'.
'Hiya, Marlene, let's get stinkin'' –
Wasn't it lovely, Glad?
Just to think of it makes you sad.
Wasn't it lovely, Glad?

Eng. Lit.

(My favourite character.) The scene is a book-lined study with stone-framed Gothic windows. A row of small painted shields are ranged along the shelves above the bookcases. There are group photographs about the room, and over the door is a pair of crossed oars. The linen chair- and sofa-covers are made from a cloth designed by William Morris. It is just possible they are original. The speaker is the wife of the Vice-Chancellor of an Oxbridge University. She wears an elderly cardigan of which she is fond. Her speech is Educated-English, well articulated, but she cannot pwonounce her Rs.

INTERVIEW

It's really very difficult to describe my grandmother. She wasn't particularly patrician but she did look

151

very like the great Duke of Wellington, only rather prettier. Just as well, really. You know, there is a picture of her in the front of my new book. I don't know – have you read my book, Mr Wimble? No, I know it is so difficult to find time to read what one really wants to. No, it was only since you have so very kindly invited me to come on to your television programme in order to discuss my book I thought – you know – that you might just possibly have read it. But I do know how it is.

Were you up at this university, Mr Wimble? Oh, how very interesting. No, I've never been there, but now I shall make a point of going . . .

No, this is *not* my first book. I've written several. Lives. They're all Lives. And the reason I have written the Life of my grandmother is because she was a remarkable woman and I liked her. She lived a very long time you know – and she never lost interest. She was what you might call *consumed* with interest till the very last gasp. And I think ninety-four is a goodly span and that is why I have called my book *The Long Result of Time* and I don't have to tell you that is Tennyson. I expect you have 'Locksley Hall' by heart, and I very much wish I had.

Yes, she was very eccentric. Very. And I think we ought to celebrate our eccentrics. It seems to me they are getting rarer and rarer. No, I don't know where they've all gone, Mr Wimble. I suppose they have been ironed out. I must say there's one thing about my grandmother: you could not have ironed her out! Oh, no – she was far too hilly.

Oh, yes, indeed, she was intellectual. Very. She came from a long line of intellectuals – father, grandfather, etcetera. I suppose the nearest parallel to my grandmother's family was the great clan of Darwins and Huxleys, and like the Darwin–Huxley lot my grandmother's family were all very much concerned with Natural Science and Genetics. And my grandmother's own particular area of interest was in the world of very small mammals.

Yes, isn't it interesting.

She had a long and very close relationship with a small red squirrel – yes, indeed, with a bushy tail! No, I've never known a squirrel at all well, but my grandmother did. And I must tell you that as well as her very strong scientific side, she was also very much concerned with reincarnation, and she was convinced that this small red squirrel was in fact the reincarnation of a much-loved cousin, who had been gathered at an earlier date. Indeed she always called the squirrel Edwin after this much-loved cousin, and I think you will agree Edwin is not a very squirrel-like name. I don't know what you should call a squirrel – Charlie, perhaps? Or if one had Greek one might call him Skyouros! I expect you have Greek. I've only got a little bread-and-butter Greek – just enough to go through Greece, but alas, in no way classical Greek.

Oh, hello, Mrs Finley. What have you got there? The evening paper? Kindly conceal it from me, dear woman, until I feel stronger and can surprise it later. Thank you. Oh, Mrs Finley – is there a favourable chance of your finding yourself in close proximity to a kettle? I think Mr Wimble and I are both very well disposed towards the idea of some tea. And something crunchy? Lovely.

Yes, my grandmother was a great dazzler.

Oh, no, don't let's talk about me. I'd far rather talk about my grandmother. Oh dear, what sort of things do television viewers want to know about one? Likes and dislikes – yes, I've got some of those. Oh, yes, I'm *very* passionate.

Well now, which do I like best – men or women? I think it rather depends what for. I am more *familiar* with men. You see, both my father and my husband were Masters of Colleges in this University, and now my husband is Vice-Chancellor, and we have four very agreeable sons, so you see, it's men, really, men all the way along the line.

I don't know what I'd have done if I'd had a daughter, but the question never arose. I do have a very frilly little grand-daughter about whom I am prejudiced. I think she's rather too aware of her appearance and her clothes for one of only six, but I find her very fetching – very.

Clothes? Oh, yes, I like clothes – on other people. Well, somehow they seem to suffer a sea-change when they get on to me. They look quite promising in the shop; and not entirely without hope when I get them back into my wardrobe. But then, when I put them on they tend to deteriorate with a very strange rapidity and one feels so sorry for them.

I tell you what I do like – *hats*! Could I, perhaps, wear a hat if I come on to your television programme? Alas, one of the things of which I am not possessed is an *in*formal hat. I fear my hats tend to be rather purposeful. Oh, well, I'll have to ask my adviser. My adviser? Oh, that's my grandson, Edward. He's only eleven, but he is *very* wise and he knows far more about the world of today than do I, and I abide by his judgment quite considerably.

I may say, Mr Wimble, that when I told him you had so very kindly invited me to appear on your television programme he said, 'Go ahead, Gaga.' (With a certain deadly accuracy he calls me Gaga!) 'Go ahead, Gaga. Live dangerously!'

I must confess this advice has somewhat unnerved me, and it prompts me to put a question to you: Mr Wimble, are you very cruel to the people who come on to your programme?

I see. And do they *like* that?

Oh, it's the *viewers* who like it . . . I wonder if I should.

Oh, thank you, Mrs Finley, we'll come and consume it instantly. In the dining-room? Right.

Tea.

Well, now I do very much appreciate your kindness in asking me to do this programme. I shall certainly consider it . . . A thought has just crossed my mind. Mr Wimble, what would happen if I were to come on to your programme and I were to be very cruel to you?

AN EVENT

Mrs Finley dear, we are out of the dining-room at long last, thank you so very much. And that was a most triumphant repast. Oh, Mrs Finley, when the time is ripe for you, we are in the market for some coffee – in here if you can manage it, thank you so much.

Now, my dear nephew, sit you down somewhere comfortable.

Yes, that really was a *very* triumphant meal.

Oh well, you see Mrs Finley has only just come to terms and made friends with our new electric cooker. It has rather a number of knobs, and it really is rather daunting. One feels one is piloting a space-craft. And for a while Mrs Finley only dared to be a Daniel about a knob called Simmer, so we had to make do with rather many meals of a tepid nature. But, now, if you see what I mean, things are hotting up, as it were.

If you are in the mood for a peppermint they are in the tin marked Edinburgh Rock. No, thank you very much. I shall try to resist.

It's very good to see you in our midst again, my dear John. How is progress doing in Africa? Oh good. One hardly dares to ask that question, for I so rarely like the answer. Progress everywhere today does seem to come so *very* heavily disguised as Chaos.

Oh John, do me a kindness and keep your eye on the time for me. There is a programme on the television that I *would* rather like you to see. It's not in the least important and we need not let it distract us unless we want it to. Perhaps you'd rather not? It's at 8.30, I think.

Oh, it's just a programme to which I faintly contribute.

Didn't you know I'd taken to going on the telly? Well that's an over-statement. I've been on it *once*. Yes, when my book about my grandmother won a literary prize. Yes, it was rather fun. This is my second venture.

There is no doubt about it, flattery does get one somewhere, and it got me on to the television. And for a while I was in grave peril owing to the great size of my head. Well, because everyone was so very nice to me and the young man who did the interview was very encouraging and so pretty. He had lovely clean hair, and he had on a psychedelic tie and, what's more, he treated me almost as if I were his equal. So you see it was very over-exciting.

Oh the programme? It's a sort of discussion programme between so-called 'intelligent people' – they get you together and then they throw you a topic.

Oh, such as 'Infidelity'. Always very popular they tell me. And 'Is Happiness Wrong?'. I don't think it is, do you? No, I rather like it.

Now and again I did find myself a little out of my depth. Well, I know so little about Elementary Sex in Schools – or was it Sex in Elementary Schools? I can't remember now, but I thought it rather a bore.

Yes, I did enjoy doing the programme; only afterwards the producer said to me, 'You are *so* natural,' as if there was a possible alternative. I felt as if I must have erred in some way; and I now feel a little self-conscious about the whole thing and I do rather dread seeing it. And I may tell you that is why I accidentally-on-purpose forgot to tell my husband, the dear Vice-Chancellor, this morning that his exhibitionist wife was going to be on the telly tonight. Because I do *not* wish to shame him in any way.

No, he won't remember. He only remembers Events if they are written down on his little Memory Jogger Pad by his remarkable secretary, Mrs Brittle. She does all his Event-remembering for him, so he doesn't have to bother.

He's dining with the Bursar – did I tell you? They've got some university business on hand. Protest, no doubt. It usually is.

The other people on the programme were tolerably agreeable. I think they were all very well known – except to me. You know there has to be something called a Fair Balance, so if you have a Labour then you have to have Tory – and we had one of each; one thick and one thin. And then if you have a man of Science, say, for special knowledge, then you have to have a Light Relief in the shape of a TV personality, and we had rather a crack-pot charmer of Scottish origin, dressed a little unusually, I thought, for one so deeply wedded to Caledonia.

Well, he was wearing an Arab burnous. No, it was never explained; nor was his relief *all* that light, come to think of it. And if you will forgive a Laurentian joke – he wasn't much of a Pillar of Wisdom either!

Oh, I was there as a *woman*. There always has

to be a woman for reasons of provocation and/or commonsense and, alas, I think I know which I was there to represent.

But, of course, *the* star of the whole thing was Dr Barstin. He's always on the programme, and you know all about him.

My dear John, where have you been? Oh yes, of course, Africa.

Well, he is a tremendous egg-head and vastly knowledgeable about a number of things without which I have managed, through a long and happy marriage, to do,

Such as the High Density of Infra-Radiation of Contra Ballic Span.

Exactly.

He is also a very, very devout agnostic, than which there are few things more bigoted. (He's a little under privileged in a number of ways.)

Oh yes, I got on with him all right until I thought he got mildly out of control on the subject of animals. People do, you know.

Mark you, I like animals – in their right place. But I do not find them as much fun as people, do you? We have our dear old hearth-rug of a dog, Hengist – or Horsa – he answers to both. I prefer people for talking to and inventing safety-pins and playing Mozart.

But Dr Barstin could not, or would not, agree.

He looked at the panel very carefully and then he said that in his opinion people were always *much* less beautiful than horses.

I quite saw his point. But I did think it was a trifle rude, and I couldn't resist saying: 'What about Greta Garbo?'

And you won't believe the depths to which he descended. He said: 'What *is* a Greta Garbo?' Laughter in court.

Can you believe it? I said: 'What a very sheltered life you must have led, Dr Barstin! You sound just like a comic magistrate in an old Ealing comedy.'

Yes, it did go down very well. There was considerable mirth. But Dr Barstin didn't like it, and he made a very cross face at me. I'm rather looking forward to seeing his cross face. Oh, it is time? Yes, turn it on. There is a knob at the side. It takes a moment to warm up, before it bursts into flower.

I think you may not recognise me when I come on because I am most unnaturally tidy. They sprayed me with some gassy substance that reduced my hair to the exact consistency of a dried loofah. I am uncannily wispless, and it stayed rigid for days.

Yes, Mrs Finley? The telephone? Oh, how tiresome. Who? My husband? To remind me to watch the programme! *Dear* man. How very nice of him. Will you please tell him I had *entirely* forgotten about it and thank him very much for reminding me. Come back and see it if you would like to, Mrs Finley, when you bring the coffee.

He is a *dear* man.

You realise, John, that Mrs Brittle must have put me down on his little Memory Jogger Pad as an Event!

Ethel

I don't understand Ethel.
I don't, I don't really.
She's one of my very best friends,
Just about the best, nearly.
She's an awfully nice girl, Ethel is,
Dainty and refined,
I mean she'd never do or say
Anything unkind.
But get her inside of a stadium
And she seems to go out of her mind.

'KILL HIM!' she yells, 'KNOCK HIS BLOCK
  OFF!'
At ice hockey or football or what.
'KILL 'EM!' she yells, turning purple,
'KILL THE PERISHING LOT!'

'SH-SH!' I say, *'ETHEL!'*
'SH-SH!' and I die of shame.
'KILL HIM AND BASH HIS TEETH IN HIS FACE!'
She says,
And she calls him a dirty name.

    I don't understand Ethel,
    I don't, I don't truly.
    She is always gentle and sweet,
    Never a bit unruly.
    She's an awfully shy girl, Ethel is,
    Wouldn't say boo to a goose.
    You wouldn't think she ever could
    Suddenly break loose.
    But get her inside of a stadium.
    And her face turns a terrible puce.

'THROW HIM OUT OF THE WINDER!' she
  yells, 'AND WIPE HIM OUT!'
And her eyes go a terrible red,
'SWIPE 'EM!' she says, looking cheerful,
'SWIPE 'EM UNTIL THEY'RE DEAD!'
'SH-SH!' I say, *'ETHEL!'*
'SH-SH!' and I nearly die,
'SWIPE HIM AND GRIND HIS FACE IN THE
  MUD!'
She says,
'AND PUT YOUR THUMB IN HIS EYE!'

I don't understand Ethel,
I don't, I don't, really.
She's one of my very best friends,
Just about the best, nearly.
She's an awfully quiet girl, Ethel is,
That's why I never see
What makes her carry on like that,
Noisy as can be.
Then last Saturday down at the Stadium
Well – it suddenly happened to me.

'BREAK HIS SILLY NECK!' I yells, 'IRON HIM
 OUT!'
Well, Ethel was startled at that.
'IRON HIM!' I says, feeling lovely.
'IRON HIM UNTIL HE'S FLAT!'
'OOH', I says, *'ETHEL!'*
'OOH', and I did feel queer.
Then she grinned, and we both of us gave a yell
'BITE A BIT OUT OF HIS EAR!'

A Terrible Worrier

Scene: the small and cosy kitchen-living-room of number 2 Alma Cottages, Bull Lane, in a rural village in Buckinghamshire. Mrs Moss lives there. Her crony, Mrs Ingstone, from number 1 next door, is a mite hard of hearing.

There he is, Mrs Ingstone. That's his car. I'd know it anywhere. It is good of him to come round so soon. Look, dear, you let him in – I know it's my cottage but you're nearer the door, and I feel funny.

Oh, there you are, Mr Molder. Come in. You know Mrs Ingstone? I was just telling her it's very good of you to come round so soon. Now, where will you sit? Will you be all right on the settee? I think it's nice for a big man. Don't sit on Kipper!

You silly old pussy-cat. Get up off that nice

settee and go and sit up on your window-sill –
there's a good boy. He likes to sit on the window-sill
and purr through the geraniums.

It's ever so good of you to come round so soon.
I've been so worried. *I haven't been able to sleep,
have I?* I told her. *I told you, didn't I?* I haven't
been able to sleep.

Mr Molder, I've done a wrong thing.

Well, we don't know how wrong, *do we?* It could
be criminal, but you don't know, do you?

I know you've got to get back to your lawyers'
office, so I'll tell you right away.

The other evening I was sitting in here when two
young people come round selling tickets for a
raffle, and I took two. No sooner did I have them
in my hand than I realised I'd done a wrong thing.

No, that's not *the* wrong thing I've done. Oh,
I've done two. Well a raffle is gambling, isn't it? I
don't like the idea of gambling – I don't mind
having a go at hoopla at a garden fête or that –
but a raffle is proper gambling. But oh! The prizes
were *lovely*!

First Prize is a cruise for two to Madeeria – there
and back. And the second prize was a cocktail
cabinet with all beautiful crystal goblets. And there
was littler prizes – a brace of pheasants and a
rabbit, and boxes of this and that and all for ten
new p.

I told Mrs Ingstone when she come back to her cottage next door that I'd got the tickets, and she said, 'Mind you win that cruise for two and I'll go with you.' We had a good laugh!

But then I started to worry.

Because I might *win*.

Well, they could make you go, couldn't they? No, I wouldn't like it, because a cruise is on the sea, isn't it? I don't like the idea of being *on* the sea. I don't mind looking at it from the side, but I wouldn't want to be on it. Well, I mean, there could be a bad storm and would there be enough lifejackets to go round? And would they expect me to undress at night? And what are you supposed to do with your dentures?

Oh, I did worry.

And then I worried about this cottage. It's a council cottage, you know, and they might think, well, if she can afford to go off on a cruise . . . you see *they* wouldn't know I hadn't paid for it. They might put up the rent, or the rates. I mean they could turn you out, couldn't they? You don't know where you are with them. I shan't vote for them next time, whoever they are.

Well, the day come for the bazaar where they was going to draw the raffle, and I'd asked Mrs Ingstone to go with me, *didn't I, but you couldn't come, could you?*

She was going to a lecture at the Women's Institute with her niece. On hormones. *But you didn't like it. Did you?* Well, they're not very nice, hormones. But did you know we was all supposed to have them? It was news to me. I don't think I've got any.

Well, I thought to meself, I'll just pop down on the bus to the Town Hall where the bazaar was and I'll just pop in and see them draw the raffle and then pop off home again on the bus. But when I get to the door of the Town Hall there was that Mrs Amblecrumbie or whatever she's called – you know, that lively little woman with the short legs, goes to St Luke's. She spots me and she says, 'Oh it's one of my Old Age Pensioners from the club. Let her in half price.' You don't mind the half price, but you don't like the attention being drawn. Still, I got a nice place up by the platform so I could see it all going on. A woman come on to do the draw, and she makes a great palaver of it, muddling up all the little ticketty bits in a container and then she puts her hand in and makes her selection.

'First prize – a cruise for two to Madeeria.'

She took all day undoing it, and I thought to meself – get on with it.

Then she opens the ticket and says 'First Prize, Lady Clutton-Taylor.'

Lady Clutton-Taylor! Well – she can afford to go on a cruise any day of the week. Nobody much clapped.

I didn't know whether to laugh or cry. I was disappointed and relieved at one and the same time. I was just bending down to pick meself up to go home when I heard my name called.

'Mrs Moss, 2 Alma Cottages, Bull Lane, a lovely rabbit.'

I looked up and there was this woman standing on the platform with a rabbit in her hand – dead – but still in its fur. Oh, I thought to meself, I'm not going to be bothered with *that*, so I won't say nothing. I'll just sit here, numb. But that Mrs Amblecrumbie . . .

'Bravo, Mrs Moss, you've won a lovely rabbit.'

Mr Molder, I had to get up out of my seat in the body of the hall and go all the way up to the platform to receive this said rabbit, and as she put it into a carrier bag for me to take off home I could see it had still got its eyes open.

No, I did *not* want it. Because you have to *do* a rabbit. No, I've never done a rabbit. Perhaps it is funny for a country woman never to of done a rabbit. Mark you, I've seen many a rabbit done. My mother must of done twelve a year if she did a dozen, and you'd be surprised what goes on under all that fur.

Well, I'm on the bus now, and I'm worrying all the time. How am I going to get rid of this blessed rabbit? I couldn't leave it on the bus because some nosey parker would come running after me, 'Oh, you've left your rabbit on the bus.' And I couldn't drop it into the gutter because it was raining. And I couldn't put it in my bin because they'd cleared it that morning, and you know what they are – once a week – if that – because they please themselves nowadays.

Oh, I did worry.

Well, I'm off the bus now, walking up Queen's Hill, and I pause to get my breath. I notice I'm standing alongside a little red car. It was parked, like, up against the kerb and its window was open about eight inches. And before I knew what I was doing I'd posted that rabbit.

As I done so a young man is coming down the hill and he says 'Good evening' to me so I know he's seen me do it. I say 'Good evening' back at him and I wait till he's out of sight and then I try the door. Locked!

I couldn't get me rabbit back.

I went up home and I didn't sleep one wink all night, *did I*? I told her. *I told you, didn't I?* Not one wink, and at first light I'm down there and the car is gone. And that's the wrong thing I done, posting that rabbit. Mr Molder, what I need to know is this: Was it an abuse of personal, private property and could any person inform against?

You don't think so?

But are you sure?

Well, that's all right then. *You won't have to come and visit me in Dartmoor, will you?*

Kipper. Don't you dare scratch that nice white paint.

No, don't move, Mr Molder. I'm going to put the kettle on and we'll have a cup of tea. He has to go out a lot now. Don't you? He's an old boy. But he knows what he's going out for, and he's going to be quick about it because it's cold out there. That's a clever boy. You hurry up and then we'll have a nice cup of tea.

Picture-Postcard

Before pin-up girls there were picture-postcard photographs of actresses on sale, and this lyric is about a showgirl in the 1914–1918 war. Skindles is the name of a riverside hotel at Maidenhead where young officers of the day took their girls. There is a legend that says no officer in the 'Blues' – the Household Cavalry – in those days was permitted to marry an actress.

> I'm the picture-postcard that your Uncle Willy
>   kept
> In his wallet, till the very day he died.
> I'm the picture-postcard that your Auntie
>   Milly found
> In your Uncle Willy's wallet,
> When he dropped it on the ground.

How your Uncle Willy frowned!
How your Aunt Milly cried!
(For she was only a bride.)
He lied, of course. He tried, of course,
Denied he'd ever known me.
He sighed, of course, and cried, of course,
Pretended to disown me.
But I'm the picture-postcard that your Uncle
    Willy kept
In his wallet till the very day he died.
While awake or while he slept,
In his wallet, ever after,
Till the very day he died.

As a showgirl I played at the Palace
In the First War, long ago.
And he was a subaltern in the Blues,
And oh! he loved me so.
But he was already promised
To the Lady Millicent Platt,
And though it seemed a pity –
That was that.
We knew at the time it was Kismet;
It wouldn't have worked, you see,
For they don't marry actresses in the Blues –
So that was that for me.
But oh! the happiness, oh! the joy;
Even now the memory kindles,

Then we parted, broken-heartedly,
One summery Sunday at Skindles.

But I'm the picture-postcard that your Uncle
 Willy kept
In his wallet till the very day he died.
While awake or while he slept,
In his wallet ever after. Till the very day,
The very day,
The very day he died.
Do you wonder how I know?
Your Auntie Milly told me so.

In the Train

The title is self-explanatory. The speaker is a friendly, endearing and chatty American, about sixty-five years old.

Pardon me?

Well, I guess this train *is* going to London. I hope so. It's where I've got to get.

Isn't this rain terrible? I've got a little plastic thing for my hat but I don't have my drizzle-boots, or a raincoat or an umbrella! I see you have an umbrella. All Englishmen carry umbrellas, don't they?

Were you at the funeral?

Yeah, it was . . . very impressive.

I didn't like it. Well, because he wasn't like that. I mean the whole thing was so – so dead. I know that's a funny thing to say, but – no, I did not like it. Is there some law over here says you have to pray on one note like they did? I mean you don't talk to your friends like that, I don't know why you should talk to God . . . I thought it was spooky.

Yeah, the flowers were beautiful. I sent some, but I couldn't find them. I hope they got there. I had the hotel fix it for me. He loved flowers, Mr Linden; he always had lovely fresh flowers in his dressing-room at the theatre. His flowers always looked like they'd really grown in the earth someplace . . . They certainly said a lot of nice things about him, that's for sure.

Yes, I did know him personally.

I met him in the United States in the war, 1945. I'm in the profession too – well, I *was*. I was a dancer. I don't suppose you ever heard of Valda and Maurice? Specialty dancers? Well, I'm Valda. Well, I took the name Valda, I'm really Vicky – Vicky Mason. Mrs Mason. What is your name? Mr Keeny? How do you do, Mr Keeny? Lovely to know you.

No, the window's fine for me, thank you. I don't want any more air. It was so cold in that church.

Yes, Valda and Maurice, specialty dancers. We were quite known in those days and Maurice was the best partner in the business. *Very* strong and he'd lift me way up – and then lower me v-e-r-y slowly. I always wore chiffon because it moves. It's the best for my kind of dancing. Ginger Rogers always wore chiffon.

Yes, it was 1945, and we were in Chicago in a show called *Hello, Helene*. Do you remember it? Had a beautiful score and a *terrible* book. They had trouble with it for weeks on the road before it opened on Broadway, and they never did get the book right, but it ran for two years! Show business!

We went to Chicago with it after it closed on Broadway, and on the Saturday morning, as the season was closing there, I had a telephone call from my feller, Bernie, in Georgia. He was in the army there, and he called to tell me he was posted to the Pacific – in 1945! The Pacific! And he was going to pass through New York City on his way, for exactly three hours on Sunday morning and he wanted me to meet him there. I hadn't seen him in months and I *had* to get to New York – it was a matter of life and death.

Let me just set the scene. Prepare to shed tears!

I am an orphan. I don't have a single relative in the whole wide world. I mean, I don't really know who I am, and Bernie was the only person in the whole world I came first with, and that's very important.

I'd been raised in an orphanage. It was a dandy

orphanage, with these cottages – nine kids to a cottage, and a cottage mother, and we had a sweet-heart of a cottage mother, a real doll, but of course none of us could come *first* with her because the turnover was too great, and you know you just want to come first with *someone*, and sometimes it happens and sometimes it doesn't, and it had happened to me. I came first with Bernie, and boy! did he come first with me! And he had this marvellous family – mother, father, brothers, sisters, uncles, aunts, cousins – the whole arrangement. And they were *darling* to me.

I don't know how it was over here in the war, but in the States you could *not* get on an aeroplane unless you had a very top priority. The Company were all going back home to New York on the train, Sunday, but I couldn't wait for that. I had to be in New York Sunday morning for this three hours with Bernie. So I said to the kids – that's the chorus girls – look, you take my heavy bag with you on the train and I'll take a little overnight bag, go out to the airport when the show is over, and get on a plane for New York. And they all said you're crazy, but, I said, I have to *try*.

So I went out to the airport and I said to the clerk, 'I need a friend.' And I told him the whole bit about I'm an orphan and Bernie is all I've got and I must get to New York.

He said, 'Are you kidding? Are you of national importance at a time like this?'

I said, 'Look, I'm an ordinary human being, and nations are made up of little people like me. Please help me,' I said, 'I'd do anything to get to New York.'

He said, '*Anything?*'

I said, 'Anything except give you my beautiful white body.' And he said, 'Next,' and I got pushed out the line!

I was so mad. 'Nobody gives a damn about people any more,' I said. 'I thought this was a war about people'; and I gave with the whole bit again about Bernie and me. You can imagine how everybody loved me!

There was this very tall man standing near me, and he was wearing a very good-looking suit of dark clerical-grey cloth. (You know I always notice detail. I noticed you have on a very beautiful black ribbed-silk tie. I can't help it. I just notice things.) This suit was a beautiful cut. Custom-made. Money! And he spoke to me in a very British accent. He said, 'Don't overdo it.'

I said, 'You don't believe me, do you?'

And he said 'Well, it strikes me as a little odd to stand here in a public place and tell everyone your entire private life.' (I do, you know. I can't help it.)

I said, 'I'm sure *you* are very important and you have an absolutely top priority because of *course* the entire world would collapse if you didn't get to New York tomorrow morning.'

He said he didn't think it would. And I said, 'I pity you. You can't tell the difference between when a person is telling the truth and when they are phoney. And you just don't care. You're all-powerful and I bet you're lousy rich, too.'

And as I said it, I recognised him! Stephen Linden, *the* British star of stage and screen. *Stephen Linden!* Can you bear it!

'Yes,' he said, 'I am quite powerful and very rich and I have a seat on the plane to New York, and you can have it.'

I said, 'You don't *mean* it? You don't even know who I am. I'm Valda of Valda and Maurice.' (I kind of hoped he might have heard of me.) And I said, 'I can pay for the ticket, I have Travelers' Checks right here.'

He said, 'Get on the plane. You can reach me at the Algonquin Hotel. Go on. Get on the plane.'

I didn't wait for him to change his mind!

And here's the irony of it. There was fog over New York and we had to divert to Philly – that's Philadelphia – and I didn't get to see Bernie for a whole *year*! And then I married him. And we have a wonderful family – three grown kids – two boys married and out of the nest, and one is still a teenager, our daughter Bernice, and here we all are in England for the very first time. It's incredible.

Well, I went round to the Algonquin on the Monday to pay for my ticket, but I didn't get to see Mr Linden, he was all tied up. I saw a very nice manager or something, but it wasn't the same thing. I was very disappointed, so near and yet so far! But of course after that I always saw all his movies, and when he was in a play I'd go to see that and then I'd go backstage afterwards and send my name in. But I don't believe he ever remembered my name, so I always said, 'Tell him it's the girl he gave his seat to on the plane in Chicago 1945.' And I always got to see him. And he was so *nice* – and he always had all these lovely fresh flowers.

We got here about ten days ago, and I hoped he might be in a show, because I'd read someplace he was part of some wonderful Repertory Company they have over here – and then I saw the news. I felt terrible. As if I'd lost a relative or something. I mean I had identified with him for so long. I wish I had known him better. Then I read in the paper where the funeral was to be down in Hampshire, and I just said to Bernie, 'You take the kids and go to a movie or see the Tower or someplace,' and I just took the train and came down.

He was such a wonderful man, and *the* most marvellous actor. Marvellous.

Did you know him personally?

You were his private secretary for thirty-five years!

Oh you must be feeling terrible, and I have talked and talked. Bernie will kill me when I tell him . . . blab, blab, blab. Oh, I am so sorry. I swear I won't say another word all the way to London. Oh, I am *so* sorry. Not a word, I promise.

You weren't the secretary at the Algonquin that time? I can't bear it!

I swear I won't speak any more . . .

Listen, if you want to talk, you just say so.

Any Messages, Mrs Bolster?

Any messages, Mrs Bolster?

Well now lets see.
Phone went when you was out
Dint say oo he was
I arst im though because
You said to dint you?
But e woont leave no name,
Seemed like a shame.

No there wasn't no message.

O, someone or other run to say
Was you goin to the meetin
Because about the seatin
I tell er I dint know

And she says O,
O I see
And she ungup on me.

No there wasn't no message.

O and a bit later on
Phome went again
And someone says 'its me'
And I says oo?
And e says you know oo darlin
And I tells im I wasn't you
You was out
And e says you can't fool me with that act
    darlin
And I says to oom do you wish to speak?
But e rungoff.
Wasn'it cheek.

No there wasn't no messages.

Time

When I was a girl there was always time,
There was always time to spare.
There was always time to sit in the sun;
And we were never done
With lazing and flirting,
And doing our embroidery,
And keeping up our memory books,
And brushing our hair,
And writing little notes,
And going on picnics,
And dancing, dancing, dancing, dancing –
When I was a girl there was always time to
    waste.

Thank the Lord.

When I was a young woman there was always
    time,
There was always time to spare.
There was always time to walk in the sun,
And we were never done
With going to weddings,
Our own and our friends',
And going to parties,
Away at weekends,
And having our children
And bringing them up,
And talking, talking, talking, talking –
When I was a young woman there was always
    time to enjoy things.

Thank the Lord.

And when I was an elderly woman there was no
    more time,
There was no more time to spare.
There was no more time to sit in the sun,
For we were never done
With answering the telephone,
And looking at the TV,
And doing baby-sitting,
And talking to our friends,
And shopping, shopping, shopping, shopping,
And washing-up, washing-up, washing-up,

Writing letters, writing letters,
Rushing, rushing, rushing,
And we were always hurried,
And we were never bored.
When I was an elderly woman
There was never time to think.

Thank the Lord.

But now I'm an old old woman,
So I want the last word:
There is no such thing as time –
Only this very minute
And I'm in it.

Thank the Lord.

First Flight

Scene: in a transatlantic aeroplane. The reason I chose for this piece a clearly defined North-Country voice is because I wanted to suggest directness, decency, naturalness and total integrity. (There is another kind of Northern voice that comes over as narrow and self-satisfied. That would not suit this sketch.)

Oh, the little light's come on.

'Fasten your seat belt' – well, I will if I can. I've had too much lunch. Can you manage?

I never saw anybody work so hard as you – all the way over, through lunch. I said to myself, 'I bet he's on a business trip.' Yes, I thought you were.

No, I'm on a holiday.

Yes, it is my first visit to America. Of course

you know just what it is going to look like, don't you. Films and television, and that. I think it's a shame really. I'd like to have been surprised. Well perhaps it will feel different when you're there.

Oh – ooh – what's that? Bumpy.

A cloud ? Oh. Yes – look – the widow's gone all white. Ah, blue again, that's better. We are coming down, you can see; yes, there it is.

It is my first flight. Well, it's not actually my *first* flight. I flew to the Channel Islands once, but I didn't like it. I came back by boat! Silly. But this is my first proper flight, with food. And I like the souvenir picture-postcard they've given us of the plane. I'm going to give it to my grandchildren; they'll have to draw lots to see who gets it.

Don't you want yours? You sure? I wasn't dropping a hint. Well, I'd love to have it if you can spare it, thank you very much. I'll tell them I sat next to a very nice man on the plane and he gave me his postcard.

I've never seen my grandchildren yet. Well, I haven't seen my son for over five years. He's in electronics. He went out on a contract, and he didn't know if he'd like it, but he did and he's settled. He's had several promotions – they think very highly of him – and when the last one came he wrote and said, 'Come on over, Mum', and he's given me the trip.

Yes, it is nice. Yes, he is, he's very bright, but he's not spoiled with it. They're going to meet me at the airport in New York. They live near a place called Stamford, Connect-ti-cutt. Oh, is that how you pronounce it? Well, I won't have to mention it when I'm there, and I can learn it for when I go home. Yes, his wife is American.

She's an Afro-American – a coloured girl.

I do hope I'll do it all right.

When the letter came I . . . I didn't really know what I thought, but I've brought up Kev – that's my son – and his sister, to believe that it isn't *who* you are – it's what you are that matters. And I really do believe that.

I suppose it's an awful thing to say, but you know in some ways I'm glad his dad . . . I lost him six years ago and he was a dear man, but he didn't like change. He liked everything to go just like it always had done. Pattern. He liked what he knew . . . I think he might have found the adjustment . . . a bit . . .

But my father! Oh my father! He loved changes if they were a good idea. And he loved people. He could always get right to the middle of a person – anybody. He was outspoken but not just for hearing his own voice. He was very well liked. He was a gardener; and he said you have lots of time to think; you put something in the ground and you have to wait for it to come up. He was a lovely man. I thought the world of my father.

I could do with having him with me here now, I can tell you . . .

I don't know whether I think it's easier for a mixed marriage in England or America. I think there's more of them in America. But I wish they were living near me, you know, with the children running in and out of the house.

But I don't know. People are very narrow where I live. They have such *little* lives. None of them use their front rooms. They've all got them and they keep them lovely but they don't live in them. Matching nets on all the windows . . . but they don't use their front rooms.

D'you know there's a woman in my Church said to me 'I don't know why you go on about us all being the same. I mean, I look in the mirror and I'm pink, and they look in the mirror and they're brown. We *are* different; we're meant to be different.'

I thought to meself 'Well, I'm glad I'm different from you.' Well, she's got some very funny false teeth. I shouldn't have said that. It wasn't kind. But she gets on my wick.

I said to her: 'Look, people are always going to look different to people, but in the sight of God we are all absolutely the same – I'm sure of it.' I hope you didn't mind me saying that? Well, people don't like you to mention God. They get all embarrassed and start counting their buttons. But I'm used to it. My father talked a lot about God.

Oh, look – we really are coming down. All those little cars – pastel coloured – pink and blue. And the back gardens – there's one with a swimming-pool and laundry. Can you see. Oh, you've seen it before.

Oh – they've put those brakes on much too fast. The whole place is shuddering. I don't like it. Are you sure it's all right? Oh there's the music come on. I'm glad to hear it. You must think me silly – oh dear . . .

Yes. There are two grandchildren, a girl and a boy. I've got lovely snaps of them – one is very, very dark, but the other . . . honestly . . . you'd never know . . . I've got lovely snaps of her, too. She's beautiful. Very tall and slim, and, of course, Kev would never marry someone who wasn't nice.

They met at a concert. He's very musical, is Kev. Opera mostly, and he has a marvellous collection of gramophone records, but of course he didn't take them with him when he went to America because he didn't know if he would settle, but he did and he sent for them. Have you ever had to send anyone a *lot* of gramophone records? Well – don't! It's awful!

She writes me such lovely letters. She calls me Mother Comstock. 'Dear Mother Comstock' – I'm Mrs Comstock you see. I think it's nice. It's got a sort of bouncy rhythm – Mother Comstock.

When I think of my mother-in-law . . . I never called her anything for twenty-five years! Except 'dear' in a time of crisis. Now and then I'd say Mrs C. and she liked it. I should have done it more often.

Do you think there is a place where they could watch for the plane coming? Observation Terraces, don't they call them, or something? They have one at London Airport I think . . .

Well, we are swinging round. There is a building coming into view with people on the roof terrace . . .

They're there.

They're all there . . .

Oh, I do *hope* I do it all right.

I just want to do it right.

I'm going to see you today

This is our red-letter-day,
It's come at last you see;
Couldn't really be a better day,
It's meant for you and me.
This day we've been awaiting, patiently.
It is perfection to me, for –

I'm going to see you today,
All's well with my world;
And the people that I meet,
As I hurry down the street,
Seem to know I'm on my way,
Coming to you.
This is a beautiful day,
I'm treading on air,
And my feet have taken to wings,

My heart with happiness sings,
I'll see you today.

The waiting days that dragged along
Were colourless and slow,
Those weary, dreary days that lagged along
As if they'd never go
Are now at last behind us, finally,
All is enchantment to me, for –

I'm going to see you today,
All's well with my world;
And the people that I meet,
As I hurry down the street,
Seem to know I'm on my way,
Coming to you.
This is a beautiful day,
I'm treading on air,
And my feet have taken to wings
My heart with happiness sings
I'll see you today.